Wolf was the most handsome man Susan had ever seen. He was also the most dangerous—and she was his prisoner. . . .

Books you will enjoy
by MADELEINE KER

OUT OF THIS DARKNESS

When tragedy struck him, Fabian Blackthorne was forced to rely more and more on Cathy Milner—and Cathy didn't mind at all. But was it much consolation to know that, in any other circumstances, he would only want Cerise Hunniford?

FIRE OF THE GODS

Photojournalism was Louise Jordan's life, so having the scoop of her career virtually handed to her on a plate was a chance she couldn't turn down—even it did mean betraying Bruno's confidence. And if he accused her of being no better than Laura Ackerman, she was still glad to have put her work first! Wasn't she?

WORKING RELATIONSHIP

In a way, Madge was thrilled to be going to Tibet with the brilliant Seton Chambers, to help him make a television documentary; she knew she would learn a lot from him. But was it worth it, when she thought of the emotional problems involved?

THE STREET OF THE FOUNTAIN

At their first dramatic meeting, in the wilds of Turkey, Rose had been almost frightened to death by the formidable Zoltan Stendahl—but it had all turned out to be a misunderstanding. Yet, now that she knew more about him, wasn't she still being deceived about his true character?

COMRADE WOLF

BY

MADELEINE KER

MILLS & BOON LIMITED
15–16 BROOK'S MEWS
LONDON W1A 1DR

First published in Great Britain 1984
by Mills & Boon Limited

© Madeleine Ker 1984

Australian copyright 1984
Philippine copyright 1985
This edition 1985

ISBN 0 263 74951 7

Set in Monophoto Times 11 on 11 pt.
01–0285 – 49293

Made and printed in Great Britain by
Richard Clay (The Chaucer Press) Ltd,
Bungay, Suffolk

CHAPTER ONE

'SUSAN Cheyne?'

'That's right.' Susie didn't bother to correct the Swiss passport official's pronunciation of her name—he'd called her *Suzanne Sheen*. For such a wealthy city, Zurich boasted a starkly functional airport, and on this summer evening, the unsmiling officials were being more thorough than Susie had ever seen them.

'You are travelling alone?'

'Yes.' The wail of a tired baby rose above the other noises of the immigration hall. The long queues of passengers from incoming flights were becoming distinctly irritable at the interminable delay, and the equally long queues already forming at the customs hall ahead of them suggested that the excise officers were being as scrupulous as the immigration people.

'You are twenty-three?'

'Twenty-two,' she corrected.

The official made a note. 'And your permanent address is in England?'

'Yes,' Susie nodded. He glanced at the photograph on the front page again, then looked up at her. Thick, raven-black hair surrounding a tanned, oval face. A generous, kissable mouth. Long-lashed eyes that were pools of dark blue. A face that was capable of heart-melting beauty.

Susie forced a tired smile, wishing he'd hurry up. The careful Swiss official relaxed slightly.

'You are a marine biologist?'

5

'Yes.' Susie nodded. 'I'm currently working for the International Geophysical Committee.'

The official made another note. 'Are you visiting Switzerland in connection with your work?'

'Switzerland doesn't have a coastline,' she reminded him rather acidly. Impatience was making her restless. Her flight had come in over an hour ago, and her father would be waiting in the Arrivals hall. 'I'm visiting my father here in Zurich.'

'His name and occupation?'

'Christian Cheyne,' she told him. 'He's the managing director of Chemical Suisse.'

'Chemical Suisse!' A flicker of respect animated the man's face. Chemical Suisse was a name that carried a lot of weight in a country which practically worshipped wealth and success. There was sudden politeness in the official's manner.

'Will you be staying with your father?' Susie nodded, and his stamp thumped approvingly on to the page. 'I hope you have a pleasant stay in Switzerland, Miss Cheyne. *Auf wiedersehn.*'

'*Auf wiedersehn,*' Susie rejoined, shouldering her bag. The official's face was already composing itself into stern lines for the benefit of the next passenger as she made her way towards customs.

She tried not to mind as they rummaged through her underwear and probed her vanity-bag. Then, with a quick scribble of chalk on her bags, she was free.

It had been six months since she'd last seen her father, and her heart was beating fast as she walked into the huge terminal beyond. She saw him instantly, tall, silver-haired, distinguished. The crowds lining the barrier had made a little space for him, out of instinctive respect.

'Daddy!'

It was a thrill to see him, and she all but ran, dragging her bags. He smelled, as always, of expensive after-shave, and his arms had lost none of their strength as he crushed her to him.

'You look ravishing.' Steel-blue eyes surveyed her proudly for a second. 'Have a good trip?'

'Oh, it's lovely to see you,' she smiled shakily, and hugged him again. She missed him, always, and these reunions were almost painful for her. He was looking good, and she told him so, feeling puppyish and absurdly young in his presence. In his charcoal suit and conservative silk tie, he carried his age with authority. A man who wore wealth like an elegant cloak, unmistakably superior, and arrogantly indifferent to others. The incised lines around his eyes and mouth creased into another smile.

'Here—these are for you.'

'Oh, Daddy——' She took the bouquet, fifteen or twenty rose-buds, perfect and dewy in sealed cellophane. The tribute, like so many things her father chose, had a curiously impersonal beauty. 'You shouldn't have.'

'You must be tired,' he said, waving away her thanks. His face, with its thin lips and hawk-like nose, was already lapsing back into the carefully neutral expression of the successful businessman. 'Let's get home for a drink. Franz will take care of the bags.' He linked his arm through hers and led her through the crowds. The chauffeur, a bulky man in uniform, followed with Susie's two suitcases.

The massive gold Rolls Royce was parked squarely outside the glass doors of the entrance.

'Wow,' Susie grinned. 'That's new, isn't it?'

'Yes.' He patted the sleek metal, studying her face for approval. 'You like it?'

'It's wonderful,' she enthused, more for his benefit than because the opulent car really appealed to her. Her father loved expensive machines like this one; they suited the demanding, efficient side of his nature to perfection.

'I bought it last month. You're welcome to use the Rolls—and Franz—while you're here,' he told her, getting in beside her. 'But I know you won't.' He patted her hand with a wry smile. 'So I've hired a little Fiat for you to use.'

'I've just never got used to things like being chauffeur-driven in a Rolls,' she said, hearing the apology in her own voice. Her father was one of the most important businessmen in Switzerland, and one of the rarest things of all—a foreigner who'd made it in the unforgiving world of Swiss high finance. It simply wasn't her world, though, and that was all.

She could easily have slid into the kind of life he'd offered her when she left school. A life of ease, of considerable luxury and privilege. But she'd never managed that. There was something too independent in her spirit, something that made her want to get out into the wide world, and use her own excellent brain. 'I love the car, Dad. It's real quality, isn't it?' She knew exactly how much the material symbols of his success meant to him. 'It suits you. It's a beauty. And thanks for getting me the Fiat—you shouldn't spoil me like this.'

'When you get to my age,' he replied obliquely, 'you'll start appreciating the luxury of being driven, instead of driving!'

Wordless as ever, Franz drove them smoothly through the concrete mazes of the airport area.

'They took ages at immigration,' she said, apologising for the delay he'd had. 'I've never seen them quite so thorough.'

'The Swiss are a thorough people,' he commented. 'I like that in them.' He glanced through the tinted window at the undeniably beautiful vista of Zurich. 'Zurich is one of the last civilised places on earth. You can really enjoy life here. Everything's laid on.'

And as if to prove his point, he'd made plans for them to eat out. There was barely time for her to glance round the lakeside villa.

'Put something smart on,' he advised. 'I'm taking you out to Spruengli's for dinner.'

'Wonderful!' Susie bubbled, and felt mean at having to force her delight. It never occurred to him, she reflected with a touch of wryness, that after six months' separation, all she wanted was a quiet evening at home with him on their first night together. To be intimate with him, and get over the first shyness. He wasn't that sort of man, though. To get close to her father, she mused, you had to stalk him like a hunter, and pounce at the right moment.

She shook off her slight sense of disorientation in the white-on-white bedroom. Yesterday she'd been taking samples of seawater along the Cornish coast, tangled and salty in sawn-off jeans. From now on, she had to be the sleek, groomed jet-setter that everyone would expect Christian Cheyne's daughter to be. She hauled her make-up bag out, and tried to cover the tiredness on her face with optimistic shades of lipstick and eyeshadow.

There were more roses in the bedroom, yellow ones, matched with Swiss precision. He loved her, yes. But he wanted to show it in his own way, using his wealth and taste, and she was going to have to accept that. At least he drove them to the restaurant himself, fast and efficiently, in the silver-grey BMW that was his other car.

'You can't imagine what a contrast this all is for me,' she smiled at him. 'I'm used to bouncing around in Land Rovers, and having sand in my hair!'

He didn't reply at first, but as they walked from the car to Spruengli's, he tucked her arm firmly under his and said, 'I want you to have a good time in Zurich, Susie. We've seen far too little of each other over the past two years. My fault, I know.'

'No, it isn't,' she said, defending him out of habit. His rise to the directorship had been a steady, twenty-year upward surge. In her early teens they'd moved from Edinburgh to Switzerland, when her father had been appointed manager of one of the biggest factories. That had been before her mother's death. Since then he'd worked with single-minded dedication, and she hated him to feel that he hadn't given her enough. 'I've been too preoccupied with my own work, Dad. Last year in Canada, and this year in England—I've let it dominate my time. When I've finished this report on coastal pollution, perhaps I'll take the leave that's due to me, and come back home to stay for a while.'

He stopped under the striped awning, and looked at her keenly. 'D'you mean that, Susie?'

'You're the only father I have,' she smiled. 'Of course I mean it.'

'Excellent,' he said in satisfaction, and led her inside.

The restaurant, stunningly expensive, and elegant in a distinctively plush Swiss way, commanded a sparkling panorama of Zurich by night. There were several business acquaintances of her father's in the place, coming up for a respectful word or two with the director of Chemical Suisse. She smiled brightly at all the introductions, and kept chattering to him through the rituals of wine-tasting and dinner-ordering which her father relished so dearly. She really wanted him to feel that he was giving her a wonderful evening.

'You're looking magnificent,' he told her over the admittedly excellent dinner. She was wearing a ruby silk dress she'd bought before leaving London, and the simple lines left her slender arms and throat bare. The raven-black sweep of her hair gave her a youthful, free look that was rather at odds with the distinctly middle-aged style and clientele of Spruengli's. 'The open-air life evidently suits you.'

'I try and stay out of the laboratories as much as I can,' she admitted with a smile.

'You're very brown.' His eyes studied her, taking in the sheen of health in her eyes, hair, and skin. 'England's having a good summer, eh?'

'Marvellous,' she nodded.

'D'you know I haven't been back since before your mother died? That's all of five years.' He poured more wine, his shrewd eyes noticing that his daughter was the object of considerable male interest from tables round about. 'Looks like you go to work in a bikini,' he suggested.

'Oh, I do sometimes. And most of the time, I'm barefoot. So far they've just let me roam free, thank God. I'm not as independent as I was in Canada last summer, but I still try and do as much research as I can on the beaches and in dinghies. I feel like a very spoiled beachcomber sometimes.'

'Sounds delightful.' His expression contradicted the words, and she had to smile. To her father, technocrat and man about town *par excellence*, wandering along a beach barefoot would sound about as delightful as lying on a bed of nails. 'As long as you're happy.'

'I'm very happy, Dad.' She held his eyes for a second, wanting him to believe her. It no longer hurt her that he had no real interest in her work as a marine biologist, but she wanted him to at least know that she was contented in her job. Which she was, very much so. Within a month she was going to have to start drawing up the report she'd been employed to write, about the effect of industry on the coastal environment.

'Good,' he nodded. She sipped the smooth wine, and glanced around the restaurant. It was filled with the sort of people her father worked with, careful-eyed Swiss in their forties, fifties and sixties, people made confident by having solid bank accounts behind them, and new Mercedes-Benzes parked outside. Their wives and mistresses had the same comfortable, respectable gloss. None of the neurotic, insecure energy she'd noticed so much in Canadians and Americans.

Her own tastes, nature-oriented and definitely modern, had little place in this money-oiled world. If she was really going to stay for a month or two when the report was finished, she was going to have to try hard to fit in.

'This place is extremely smart,' she volunteered, wanting to please him. 'And the food's delicious.'

'I eat here regularly,' he nodded, turning to his *jaegersnitzel*. 'They know me.' She didn't comment. Since her mother's death, he'd delegated large areas of his life out to employees. A housekeeper kept the big villa on the lake as scrupulously clean as an estate-agent's show-house. Gardeners kept the grounds immaculate. He ate in restaurants, was driven by a chauffeur, allowed his secretary to take care of all his social arrangements.

Maybe parcelling his life up in neat contracts like that was his way of dealing with the loneliness of widowerhood, she thought sadly. She'd have liked him to marry again, some kind, supportive Swiss like the women in the restaurant tonight, but he was an essentially private man, and she knew that he'd probably find the idea impossible. Lorna Cheyne had been an exceptional woman, and maybe, in some crazy way, he was still being faithful to her memory. Dealing with servants, burying himself in his work, these were ways of staying uninvolved. Of avoiding pain.

'If I *do* come and stay,' she said, 'I hope you'll give the housekeeper a holiday.'

'Whatever for?' he asked in surprise.

'You look like Cary Grant when you raise your eyebrows like that,' she teased. 'Because I shall want to look after you myself, that's why.'

'Is that so?' He smiled slightly. 'The international scientist? Don't tell me you're becoming a homebody in your old age.'

'I want to play the dutiful daughter, that's all. Darning socks and making wholesome soups.'

'Can you cook?' he enquired. His surprise made Susie pout.

'Come on, Dad—I'm not *that* unworldly.'

'But you are very much a liberated girl of the late '80s,' he said, dabbing his mouth with the napkin.

'Is that the way I seem?' she wondered, pausing to watch his face.

'You've got a degree. You have your own job. and by your own admission you enjoy it thoroughly. You're successful, too. People in your profession respect your opinions. You get asked to do important surveys on technical subjects. You live alone.' He quirked an eyebrow at her. 'I *trust* you live alone?'

'I do,' she grinned, unembarrassed.

'You travel round the globe, think nothing of sleeping in a tent on a lonely beach —' He poured her more wine. 'In my book, that adds up to a very liberated life, Susie.'

'I suppose it does,' she nodded.

'I think you're very brave, and I'm proud of you. That doesn't stop me from worrying. Yes,' he smiled, holding up a hand to stop her assurances that she was doing fine, 'I know you can take care of yourself. You think I want to cosset you, keep you here in a golden cage. I just want to protect you from being hurt. You've gone a long way, Susie. You're doing things that your mother, for example, would never have dreamed of.'

'I know,' Susie nodded. 'Yet I never thought of Mum as not being liberated.'

'Your mother was one of the happiest people I've ever known.' If there was grief in his ice-blue eyes, she couldn't detect it. 'Lorna was a traditional woman. And we had a traditional marriage. Neither of us were free. And I mean that in the best possible way, because neither of us *wanted* to be free. We were utterly committed to each other.'

'I know,' Susie said softly.

'It's just that you've traded the things you could have had—like security, comfort, a relatively luxurious lifestyle, a husband who'd take care of you—for freedom.'

'I hope I haven't traded away my chances of getting a husband,' she smiled, but there was a tug of uneasiness somewhere inside her. It had occurred to her before that she was, indeed, living a very different life from her mother's. 'Times have changed,' she sighed. 'I wouldn't respect myself if I didn't do *something* with my life.' After two years in the field, she tended to think of herself as an experienced old trooper. In reality, though, her career was in its very early stages, and though all had gone well so far, she knew that there was much to come yet. She tended to think of the future rosily, telling herself she'd cope. Her father had a way of challenging those assumptions!

'Doing something with your life might mean bringing up happy, well-adjusted children,' he pointed out mildly.

'And stroking some man's vulnerable ego for the rest of my life,' she suggested drily. 'Entertaining his boss, and washing his underwear, and keeping his house spotless.'

'Well,' he reminded her, 'haven't you just volunteered to do all that for me?'

'I can see why your board of directors are all terrified of you,' she said ruefully. 'All right, Dad—I have to admit that the domestic life has an attraction for me. It must be some deep female instinct, I guess. But I'd have to be very much in love with the man to sentence myself to the kitchen sink when I could have the whole Atlantic Ocean!'

He laughed, and dropped the subject at that point. But when they got back to the villa, around eleven, he paused on the patio that overlooked the lake, and put his hand on her shoulder.

'You must have a dozen gorgeous young men chasing after you, Susie.' The statement, as she well knew, was a question, and she grinned.

'I've just met a *rather* gorgeous young man,' she admitted. 'Want to hear about him?'

'If there's the remotest chance that he could persuade you to trade the Atlantic for a sinkful of dishes,' he replied.

'I wouldn't have to,' she chuckled. 'Joe's the head of the marine research station at Fairbourne.'

'Another marine biologist?'

'A PhD,' she nodded. 'Joe Dowson. He's quite a lot older than I am, and a better scientist than I'll ever be.'

'And he's serious about you?'

'It's a little early to tell.' She thought of the affectionate brown eyes, so meltingly tender. 'We only met a few weeks ago. But I like him a lot, and he wants——' She just couldn't stifle her yawn of sheer tiredness. 'Sorry! He wants to see more of me when I get back.'

'An understandable wish,' her father said gently, kissing her forehead. 'You'd better get some sleep, kid. You're worn out. You can tell me all about Joe tomorrow.'

'It's wonderful to be here, Dad,' she told him warmly, hugging him goodnight. 'And about coming to stay at the end of the year—I mean that. I really do.'

Susie blinked into wakefulness as the curtains were drawn, letting summer brilliance into the white bedroom. The housekeeper, a formal but pleasant German-Swiss in her fifties, turned to her with a smile.

'*Guten tag, Fraulein*. Welcome back to Zurich. You have slept well?'

'Rather too well,' Susie said, sitting upright and glancing at her clock. It was already past ten. 'Thank you for waking me, Magda. It's good to see you again.'

'And good to see you, *Fraulein*.' Magda had served her father for the past three years, and Susie had always liked her.

'Has my father gone to work yet?'

'Herr Cheyne left for the office at eight. I did not wish to wake you—you must have been tired after your journey. What would you like for breakfast?'

'Please don't worry—I'll make myself something in a minute.'

'I have already prepared cereals and coffee,' Magda smiled. 'Shall I unpack the Fraulein's bags?'

'Oh, no.' Embarrassed, Susie shook her head. 'Thank you, Magda—I'll see to all that.' She didn't want Magda running around after her, but knew that the Swiss housekeeper would feel she was failing in her duty if she didn't make Susie welcome. 'But I'd be very grateful for coffee and cereal. I'll be down in ten minutes.'

Magda left, and Susie clambered out of bed to have a shower. The sizzling jet of hot water was delicious on her naked skin, and she revolved under the spray, trying to keep her hair dry.

The little suite had so obviously been designed with Susie in mind. A rather vainer Susie than she really was, she smiled, stepping out of the shower and catching sight of herself in the full-length mirror fixed to the tiled wall. Her breasts, pale against the rich tan of the rest of her body, were high and proud, their firm nipples arrogantly sexual, and almost as dark as the triangle between her thighs. Gold on cream, she stepped on to the mat and towelled herself dry. She wasn't self-conscious about her body, perhaps because of the past two summers spent under blazing suns, but she was always grateful to have inherited her mother's slimness.

She was taller than her mother had been, though, long-legged and taut-muscled. As she stretched up to gather her raven hair, her breasts lifted into perfect relief, and the line of her ribcage was clear under the silky skin. A lush body, she was forced to acknowledge. Oh, for that summer last year, when hard living along the Nova Scotia coast had honed her figure down to bony efficiency!

She considered her shortish, unvarnished nails, and reflected that she was going to have to polish her exterior rather more than she was used to. Her father was going to be introducing her to his colleagues and friends this holiday, people · he respected, and he'd want her to look suitably groomed. Nail varnish, more make-up, and an appointment with a good hairdresser were the least she'd have to undertake. She didn't exactly mind, but it wasn't really her scene. That was one of the nice things about Joe—he didn't expect her to look like a *Vogue* model all the time. In fact, he seemed to prefer the beachcomber look!

She dressed, picking a white linen frock in honour of the splendid weather, breakfasted frugally, and took a walk to the shore of the lake.

Summer in Switzerland, Susie reflected peacefully, was even more beautiful than winter. Alpine pastures seemed all the lusher for the white austerity that had clothed them in winter; the grass was now a rich golden-green, and only the highest peaks beyond the lake were still inlaid and filigreed with snow, picture-postcard summits against a flawless blue sky.

She walked through the neat grounds, enjoying the summer warmth and the delicious air, which still seemed to hold a champagne-fresh hint of distant snows. She was thinking about last night, and the conversation she'd had with her father. He had been looking so well, better than she'd seen him since her mother's death five years ago.

Moments of tenderness like last night's good-night hug were very precious to her. Their conversation over dinner had been more intimate and personal than they were used to. Her father, she had to admit, was a materialist. Not *materialistic*, simply not emotional. More comfortable with figures and machines than with the unpredictable human vagaries of people.

'More Swiss than the Swiss,' her mother had once joked. 'Christian can sometimes make a computer seem positively sentimental.' There hadn't been any resentment behind the words. Christian Cheyne's love for his wife and his only child was sincere, for all it wasn't demonstrative. It was a love that came from deep in his spirit, almost too deep to allow for much demonstration.

Susie glanced at the glass-fronted Chemical Suisse tower, glinting among the distant buildings of Zurich across the lake. An Englishman like Christian Cheyne, superbly efficient though he was, would always have the disadvantage of being an outsider in this essentially small, tightly knit, and highly competitive community.

The cold reserve, which had deepened even

further since the death of Lorna Cheyne five years
ago, was partly a defence mechanism which helped
him survive as the managing director of one of
Switzerland's most successful chemicals companies.
The newly built glass tower was the centre of a
network of plants and factories that extended
throughout Europe. A cut-throat world, in which
any weakness would be exploited and turned to
advantage.

Maybe with Joe by her side she'd be able to get
closer to her father again? It was pleasant to
imagine Joe's warmth touching her father—but
not very realistic. She had to admit that Joe's easy-
going gentle ways were a million miles from her
father's steely strength.

She herself had very little of her father's
coldness in her. Her emotions were mobile,
instinctive. She tended to trust her heart over her
head. Not exactly a scientific trait, but she'd
inherited enough of her father's keen, disciplined
intelligence to have become an excellent biologist.
And three years of university, plus two of full-time
work, had matured Susie into the full flush of her
womanhood. A womanhood that was a darkly
beautiful echo of her mother's—adult in mind,
raven-haired and sweet-faced, with a long-legged
and high-breasted body whose elegant lines could
become almost angular when she lost more than a
few pounds.

She walked back to the villa. The breakfast-
room was empty, the table just as she'd left it, with
her bowl and cup still not cleared away. That was
unlike Magda, Susie thought wrily—she normally
had tables cleared and polished almost before the
diners had walked out of the room.

Feeling in the mood for more coffee, Susie

walked into the kitchen. A sugar-bowl lay smashed on the floor, its contents strewn around. Susie raised her eyebrows, and was about to smile at this further un-Magda-like detail, when she saw the smashed plates in the sink.

And the big Moulinex food-mixer, lying on its side on the floor, its stainless-steel bowl deeply dented.

Her heart began to pound for some reason she couldn't explain. Something was wrong in the house, badly wrong.

'Magda!' she called, and ran through into the big reception room. 'Magda! Are you all right?' The room was empty. She burst through the study door. 'Magda?'

She saw them simultaneously. Magda, bound and gagged on the floor, her face to the wall—and the tall man who was already moving towards her, fast.

CHAPTER TWO

Susie screamed in blind terror, clawing at his face. He swung her round easily, his hand a steel vice round her wrist. The Persian rug beneath her slipped on the polished floor, and she lost her balance. He didn't let her fall, jerking her ruthlessly to her feet, and dragged her out into the hallway.

'Let me go!' she gasped, terrified half out of her wits. He was unbelievably strong, a lean, tall man whose dark tan matched her own. He wore a cheap black leather jacket and a workingman's soft cap. Vivid green eyes met hers fiercely from under black brows.

'No noise.' She'd seen guns in films, but the black automatic pistol was immense as he pointed it between her eyes. The muzzle gaped hungrily, and she shrank back with chilled veins. 'Now come.'

He hustled her to the door, digging the gun into her ribs to remind her of its presence. Her mind was whirling in the total bewilderment of terror as he forced her on to the drive outside.

The big Mercedes-Benz estate car had been waiting at the entrance to the drive, and it roared forward with a spray of gravel. Susie felt his iron hands thrust her forward as one of the back doors swung open. Then she was being slammed on to the floor, face down between the front and back seats. She screamed again, desperately, hoping someone would hear her, send for help; and then the Mercedes accelerated forward hard. The man with the gun forced her back on to the floor as she tried to sit up. The cold steel of the muzzle banged into her cheekbone.

'Don't move,' he commanded savagely. 'Or I'll blow your head off.'

She lay in trembling silence, her dark hair tumbled wildly around her face. Had they killed Magda? No, they wouldn't have bothered tying her up if she'd been dead. Thank God for that, at least. Was this a kidnap? Again, an unreal sense that this was all a film came over her. A kidnap. It couldn't be anything else. Dust from the floor of the car made her cough painfully. When she tried to ease her arm, agonisingly twisted under her, the gun touched her temple again.

'I won't warn you again,' he said icily. 'Lie still.' She lapsed into immobility. She could see nothing but the floor carpet and one of his boots, the black leather well-worn.

She lay like that for over half-an-hour, numbed with fear, hearing nothing but the roar of the engine underneath her.

Zurich wasn't a big city. By now they would be in the countryside. And her father would be sitting in his office, utterly unaware that anything was wrong.

When finally the car jerked to a stop, she was almost crippled with cramps. The gunman pulled her upright, and pushed her out of the door. She was forced to lean on the arm he offered her, and her face was white with pain and shock as she stared at the small farmhouse. It was slightly derelict-looking, set in big meadows with cows and black-faced sheep. There was a reception committee waiting in the yard.

Two men in their late twenties, and a blonde girl who looked about eighteen. All were dressed in casual, slightly shabby clothes, like students or ordinary young working people. All had a slightly unkempt appearance, as though they kept their hair and faces deliberately crumpled to make recognition and remembrance difficult. All moved with the same frightening intentness of purpose as they took charge of Susie, and led her into the farmhouse.

'*Benvenuto,*' the taller of the men said quietly, locking the door behind them. His eyes flicked expressionlessly over Susie's pale face. '*É andato bene?*'

'*Si,*' the gunman nodded. He uncocked the pistol he'd been carrying, and laid it on the plain pine table. Other weapons, pistols and sub-machine-guns, were in evidence. Susie, sick and feeling horribly vulnerable, stared at their faces. The blonde girl slid her arm round the gunman's waist, and leaned up to kiss his cheek.

'Clever Wolf,' she said softly. She pronounced the name in the German way, with a hard 'V', and to rhyme with 'golf'. Her eyes were a pale china-blue, the coldest eyes Susie had ever seen in a woman's face. She turned them on Susie now, and smiled. The eyes were like openings cut into a pretty doll's mask, openings that revealed an Arctic wilderness beyond. 'Little Miss Cheyne,' she said in the same soft voice. 'How nice to make your acquaintance.'

'There isn't much time,' one of the young men said urgently. 'Come and eat, Wolf.' The gunman nodded, turning indifferently away, and the burly driver took Susie's arms in a vice-like grip, thrusting her roughly through into the next room.

Susie gasped as she stumbled across the threadbare carpet, and the blonde laughed.

'On the chair,' she commanded. Her voice was slightly accented, French or German, Susie couldn't tell. As the driver pushed her on to the hard wooden chair, she caught sight of the enamel bowl and the scissors that lay on the carpet in front of her.

'What are you going to do to me?' she asked breathlessly. The china-doll face was amused, a greedy smile on the pursy little mouth.

'Are you frightened, *liebchen*?' she asked. The scissors glittered in front of Susie's eyes, and she shrank back in horror. The driver's ruthless hands forced her to sit still as the blonde leaned forward. Susie shut her eyes as the scissors began slicing through her long, dark hair. Bewilderment was numbing her, like a succession of body-blows. 'We're going to shave you bald, *liebchen*,' the soft little voice said gloatingly. 'That's what they do to traitors and informers in Belfast, not so?'

'I haven't betrayed anyone,' Susie said helplessly, closer to tears than she'd been throughout her ordeal. The soft curls were falling into her lap and on to the shabby carpet as the blonde chopped, and the driver's fingers were biting into her shoulders cruelly. What in God's name was this all about?

'You have betrayed the working classes of the world,' the driver said thickly. 'You and your class have had your heel in the face of the people for long enough.'

Susie gasped out loud as the scissors tore unfeelingly at her hair.

'You feel the pain?' the girl said pleasantly. The

scissors wrenched viciously at the fine hair of her temples. 'So. The realities of life are beginning to break through your privileged little shell at last.'

'Careful, Senta,' the driver rumbled. 'Wolf said she was not to be harmed—and you spoil her hair like that.'

The points of the scissors pricked Susie's neck hard, close to the jugular. Susie held her breath, waiting for the blow that would bring the blood spurting out of her body.

'Just a tickle, *lieber* Udo, just a tickle. This creature and her kind have been torturing and exploiting for centuries.' But the cutting became neater, more efficient, the sharp scissors cropping Susie's raven hair into some kind of short style. 'And a little pain is excellent for ensuring discipline.'

Misery and bewilderment engulfed Susie in an inner tide. Was this a horrible dream from which she was going to awaken, relieved and unharmed? The fine hairs clung to her eyes, sticking to her cheeks where sweat made her skin moist. No dream, but an unbearable reality.

'Very good.' The quiet, authoritative voice was instantly recognisable. Susie opened tear-blurred eyes. The gunman was leaning against the doorpost, eating a crusty sandwich. He had taken off his cap and jacket, and through her tears she could see that his hair was dark and close-cut, his face hard and tanned. Eyes as green as a leopard's, watchful against the golden skin. 'You should have been a hairdresser, Senta,' he observed. 'I can just see you in some bourgeois ladies' *salon*.'

'With a machine-gun in my hands,' the girl called Senta agreed. She tilted Susie's cropped head briskly. 'Enough?'

'Excellent,' he nodded. He was tall and lean, the T-shirt clinging to the tapering line of his taut waist.

'What did you do to Magda?' Susie asked, her voice catching on raw nerves.

Senta's slim fingers wrenched sharply at her hair, breaking the words off on a cry of pain.

'You see, Wolf, she needs discipline.'

'Time for that later,' Wolf said mildly. 'Get her ready now. And don't hurt her.'

'Sure,' the soft little voice cooed. Her fingers were still locked in Susie's hair, and through her pain she could imagine the greedy look in the icy blue eyes.

'Senta.' The authority in the deep voice was unmistakable. 'Don't hurt her.'

'Sure,' Senta repeated sulkily. But the fingers relaxed their hungry grip. The man called Wolf was obviously a leader, someone whose authority meant much in the little group in whose hands her life now lay. He nodded calmly, and walked out again.

Susie slumped tiredly in the chair, listening almost without interest to the sound of Senta filling the basin behind her. She should be memorising all the details, memorising the faces for future reference—but her senses felt stupid. The farmhouse looked poor but used. No doubt it belonged to people who sympathised with whatever dark cause motivated her captors, people who would cover for them, and deny all knowledge when questioned.

'Hold her, Udo.' Susie's tired muscles tensed as the driver's paws thrust her forward. The basin which Senta was holding in rubber-gloved hands was full of a clear liquid. The smell which came off it was horribly familiar.

'No!' Susie screamed, but Udo grabbed her hair, and forced her head down into the basin despite her struggles. The warm liquid hissed against her scalp, flooding her nostrils with a sickly, dry, brown-paper smell. Peroxide of hydrogen. Made strong enough to fizz and bubble in her hair.

Susie kicked madly, clawing at the hands that held her. Peroxide splashed over her clothes, into her nose, scalding her eyes. The hands rammed her head down into the basin again, and bitter sobs exploded out of her tortured lungs at last. Her strength seemed to gush out of her with the tears, and she was dimly aware of Senta's tinkling laugh as her resistance died. She cried quietly and painfully as they worked the bleach into her hair, holding her in her crouching position for long minutes, soaking her cropped hair in the basin. Some memory dredged up the helplessness of once at school, when four or five of her friends had held her down and tickled her until she yelled for mercy. Except that this was a darker deed. It had a deadly, cruel purpose, a purpose she couldn't yet fathom.

In the end, they released her, and gave her a coarse towel to mop her face with. The sickly smell of the bleach clung nauseatingly in her nostrils and in the limp curls of her hair. The driver silently refilled the basin with water, and put it in her lap.

'Wash your hair now,' he commanded in his gravelly voice. 'Or the chemical will burn your skin.'

Clumsily, slowly, Susie slopped the water over her hair. It felt terribly short beneath her fingers, and her body ached from where she had hurt herself in her wild struggles. Some of her fingernails were broken.

From deep inside her spirit, she tried to draw up some reserve of strength and courage. She'd been through ordeals before, though never like this. But research on the coastline of Nova Scotia had forced her to face fierce weather and killer seas often enough. And she'd had to bear grief before. She must do so now, bear it and be patient, no matter what they did to her.

She looked up blearily as Senta took the basin from her.

'Little capitalist bitch,' she said softly, pale eyes hungry for Susie's pain. 'If I had my way, you would be taught a lesson that would stay with you for the rest of your life. So be warned, *liebchen*—from now on, you do what we tell you.' There was a livid scratch on the girl's pale forearm, and Susie exulted inwardly at having taken a tiny revenge on her captors.

Senta switched on the hairdryer, and raked a comb through Susie's hair. The heat was set too high for comfort, scorching the already tender skin of Susie's scalp, but she bit back her pain. She wasn't going to give Senta the enjoyment of seeing her suffering, if she could help it.

Above the whirr of the hairdryer she heard the sound of some kind of lorry or big truck pulling up outside. She paid the sound no attention; she'd suddenly noticed a telephone in one corner of the sparsely furnished room. If she could get to it for a few seconds, just to get through to her father and warn him of what had happened——

Her heart was beating faster as Senta snipped at her hair again, tidying up some final strands. Studiously, she avoided looking at the 'phone. Udo, the driver, was in the next room, and she could hear the murmur of voices as they apparently greeted the newcomer, whoever he was. Seconds would be enough, if the blonde girl left her alone.

'So.' Senta tossed a little pocket-mirror into her lap, and unplugged the hairdryer. 'Look at yourself now, *liebchen*.' Susie peered dazedly into the square of glass.

Unrecognisable. The pale face that stared back at her with haunted ultramarine eyes was framed by a page-boy fringe of dirty blonde hair. Her whole appearance had altered—and though it was obvious from close by that her hair had been clumsily bleached, she knew that from any distance she would be a common, short-haired blonde. *That* was what they'd been trying to do—transform her appearance!

She blinked away tears for the glossy black tresses that now lay scattered around her ankles. The violation of her hair was a minor incidental. She'd need her courage for more serious things from now on.

'Disappointed?' Senta sneered. 'At least the police pigs won't spot you so easily now. Later we will complete the bleaching.' Susie looked up at the girl's face. Absently, she calculated that this taut little doll must be at least three years younger than herself. A doll from a nightmare, with the slim body and blonde prettiness of a tennis prodigy, and the empty eyes of an experienced killer. But the china-doll façade no longer fooled Susie. This girl was lethal, someone who enjoyed inflicting pain and humiliation, who knew how to use them as weapons.

Senta laughed at Susie's expression, and held out her hand for the mirror.

'Give. We don't want you cutting that pretty throat, do we?'

'There's nothing you could do to me that would drive me to that,' Susie said through clenched teeth, surrendering the mirror. Senta turned scornfully away, and walked through into the next room.

Shakily, Susie rushed for the telephone, and lifted the receiver as quietly as she could. What the hell was the number for the police? Damn, damn. She didn't know. Her fingers were trembling as she dialled the number of her father's office, her ears straining for the sound of discovery.

She didn't hear the footsteps behind her, but the hand which chopped the receiver down moved with a familiar swiftness.

She whipped round to stare up into the bronzed, harsh face of the man who had brought her here at gunpoint. His eyes were as clear and cold as the depths of cabuchon emeralds. Eyes that looked indifferently on violence and death.

'Silly Miss Cheyne,' he said softly. The eyes probed her mind like lancets for a second, invading her thoughts. Then he pushed her backwards, hard. 'Get back to the chair. *Quick.*'

Susie sprang back to the chair with thumping heart. What punishment was he going to mete out now?

'Senta! Udo!' His bark brought the other two into the room, the driver holding a pistol in one meaty hand.

There was contempt in the powerful line of his body as he confronted them.

'Is this how they trained you in El Marada?' he asked silkily, his voice like a lash. 'To leave an intelligent and resourceful captive alone with a telephone?'

Senta's pale eyes darted from the telephone to Susie.

'Has she used it?' she asked tensely. 'By God, I'll cut her tongue——'

'Had she attempted to use it,' Wolf said quietly, 'I would have already killed her. As for your unforgivable carelessness, I would have killed both of you.' The cool certainty in the promise was breathtaking. The driver's fleshy face flushed crimson, then paled. Senta's expression did not change. She glanced at the silvery eyes of the man called Wolf, and shrugged.

'She would not have had the courage,' she said sullenly. 'It is of no account.'

Wolf's hard mouth stretched in a humourless smile. 'Perhaps we shall leave the Executive Committee to decide whether such gross carelessness is of account or not.'

Senta's gaze slid away from his now, an ugly fear creeping into the china-blue eyes.

'I acknowledge my carelessness, Comrade,' Udo said, his rough voice stammering slightly. 'It won't happen again.'

Wolf nodded curtly, and Susie let out an inward gasp of relief as Senta turned on her heel and walked swiftly out. He had deliberately shielded her from the retribution the others would certainly have wreaked on her. Why? She looked up to find the icy eyes on her face again, as though reading the thoughts that were passing through her brain.

The threat in them was unmistakable.

He had obviously decided that she had now learned her lesson. And if she hadn't, the malachite-hard eyes were promising there wouldn't be another chance. Wolf wielded power here. That was something to remember well. But who or what were the Executive Committee?

Udo glanced at his watch, then cleared his throat uncertainly.

'It's one o'clock, Comrade Wolf.'

Wolf nodded, and lifted a square airline bag off the table. He dropped it into Susie's lap.

'Put these on,' he commanded. She peered inside at the worn jeans and T-shirt that were neatly folded on top of a lightweight zip-fronted jacket in cheap green plastic. There were also some simple, used-looking underthings. She looked up at Wolf.

'I refuse,' she said stubbornly. There was no answering glint of anger in the splendid green gaze.

'I am surprised by your foolishness, Miss Cheyne,' he replied gently, as though dealing with an unreasonable child. 'But there are always alternatives for foolish people.' There was a black pouch like a pencil-case on the table, and he flicked it open for her to see the gleaming hypodermic syringe that lay ready-filled inside. A narcotic, something that would turn her into a limp parcel for convenient transportation. 'I should prefer to do without this. And you?'

Susie was feeling sick as she stood up, and slowly pulled the clothes out of the bag. These people weren't simply psychopathic monsters. They were an extremely dangerous and highly trained team, carrying out what was clearly an immaculately planned operation. Her puny resistance would only ensure ruthless force in return. Udo's glistening eyes were hungry on her slim body, and her mouth quivered in disgust as she took the clothes out of the bag.

Wolf smiled slightly.

'Udo. Check that the maps are in order.' With a disappointed grunt, the big man shambled out,

and the smile was still in place on the deeply
carved mouth as his eyes returned to Susie. 'Don't
waste time, Miss Cheyne.'

Susie eased her sandals off slowly, with gritted
teeth. Hadn't they humiliated her enough?

'I don't suppose it would mean anything if I
asked you for some privacy?' she said in a low
voice.

'Not after your recent display of ingenuity,' he
said silkily. 'Please don't delay, or you will simply
afford Senta another opportunity for the—shall I
say correction?—which she so enjoys.'

The threat forced her to obey. As she fumbled
with the buttons on her white dress, bought
especially for the holiday, her cheeks were burning
dully. She was wearing minimal summer underclothes, the bra and briefs almost transparent. She
felt, rather than saw, his eyes on her tanned body
as she folded the dress over the chair, hating him
for what he was doing to her pride.

'You can leave your underwear,' he ordered
curtly. 'Save the others for later.'

Later? She dressed hastily to cover her body, her
eyes averted. She tugged the jeans on first,
loathing the unmoved authority with which he was
controlling her life. They were tight, hugging her
hips and thighs, but at least they were clean. The
T-shirt was small for her, and couldn't be properly
tucked into the waistband of the jeans.

'And the jacket.'

The cheap plastic was stained with coffee and
grease. She didn't have to look in a mirror to
know that she was now unrecognisable as the
raven-haired, well-dressed Susan Cheyne who had
arrived at Zurich airport last night. She flinched as
he reached for her throat, but his sure fingers were

only going for the clasp of the gold cross and
chain she wore. It had been her last birthday
present from her father, and she couldn't bear to
lose it. 'Please,' she begged, clutching at his hands.
'My father gave this to me——'

He was very close, close enough for her to smell
his man-smell and see the tiny wrinkles at the
corners of his startlingly beautiful eyes. His face
was strong, its lines uncompromising, frighteningly
masculine. His skin was warm under her fingers.

As though he hadn't heard her plea, he tugged
the thin chain loose. But he slipped the slim cross
off it, and put it into her hand.

'Thank you,' she whispered, her fingers closing
gratefully over the scrap of gold that meant so
much to her.

'Now come.' He gave her the airline bag, which
now contained only a change of underwear. 'Take
this.' There hadn't been a flicker of emotion in his
hawked face. With a stab of acid realisation it
occurred to her that the gesture of giving her
back the cross had been mathematically computed
to encourage her co-operation.

'I haven't any shoes,' she pointed out.

'Which will discourage you from running away,'
he remarked calmly. The clothes felt unfamiliar as
she walked ahead of him into the next room, the
jeans far tighter than she would ever have chosen
to wear.

There was an atmosphere of intent activity now,
but she had no time to glance at the people in the
room, which was filled with cigarette-smoke. Udo
grabbed her arms, and hustled her out of the door
into the brilliant summer sunlight. The beautiful
Alpine slopes mocked her from under a blue sky.
Stones dug sharply into the bare soles of her feet.

Her grunt of pain prompted Udo to growl, 'The children of Palestine have no shoes.'

Beside the car was now a large freight-truck, the sides of its van painted with the emblem of Motta, the huge Italian confectionery firm. Stolen, or more likely forged, she guessed.

One of the young men was waiting by the open tail-gate. Panic made Susie struggle fiercely as they forced her up the ramp, a terror of being enclosed. Udo cuffed her heavily again, knocking her almost senseless. A push sent her sprawling into the back of the truck. As Udo and the other man began closing the doors and bolting them from the outside, she picked herself dazedly up, taking in her surroundings in a frightened glance. The truck was half-full of crates and boxes, bound with steel tape and packed in straw, and stamped with the Motto logo; but there was a mattress in one corner, two blankets, and an airline bag like the one still slung over her own shoulder. She turned to the men, terrified of the dark and the confinement of her prison.

'Please!'

The tail-gate slammed shut, leaving her in total darkness. The bolts rammed shut outside like gunshots.

Her childhood claustrophobia rose up in a horrific wave, and she staggered over to the doors, banging on them hysterically.

'Don't leave me in here! *Please!*'

The silence echoed. The walls of the van were double-thicknesses of steel, designed to insulate and protect a delicate cargo. And, incidentally, to prevent any sound from within from reaching the outside. Fighting back tears, she groped her way over to the mattress, found it, and curled up on the bare comfort it afforded, pressing the rough blanket to her mouth, feeling the panic beginning to scream inside her.

What was she facing? Death, perhaps unbearable pain and humiliation?

She buried her face in the rough wool, grasping for courage. There was no doubt in her mind that they wanted money. Christian Cheyne was a rich man, the commander of a huge company. For his daughter's life, this little gang could ask millions. And it didn't matter whether they wanted the money to buy weapons for some mad cause, or for pure personal greed. Within days, maybe even hours, complicated negotiations were going to begin. The process she'd read about so often, seen so often on the television screen, and never even thought about. The weighing-up of money and honour, principle and precedent, against the value of a single human life. Police, lawyers, Chemical Suisse directors, political spokesmen of both sides.

And in those negotiations, she knew, her own feelings and those of her father were going to count less than sparrow's tears.

There was a distant bang like a door closing, and then the truck's powerful engine exploded into life. The deep vibration seemed to go through the walls of her chest, despite the insulation of the mattress. A jolt, and then they were moving.

Down the farm road, past the scented meadows and the incurious cows, under a brilliant sun.

CHAPTER THREE

SHE lay in the total darkness, listening dimly to the roar of the truck's engines beneath her body. Her prison smelled vaguely of chocolate and straw, but it was reasonably cool. The darkness, after the shock of the past few hours, was producing a sense of weird unreality in her mind, and her head was aching abominably. She had always hated the dark, ever since childhood. It was one of her few phobias.

The strip lighting along the sides of the van flickered into life suddenly, and she picked her head up vaguely.

'Miss Cheyne.' She blinked round the walls for the origin of the metallic voice. There, a speaker-grille, set behind the driver's cab, high up against the ceiling.

'Miss Cheyne. Can you hear me?'

'Y-yes,' she called, raising her voice above the noise of the engine. 'Please—let me out of here!'

'I'm afraid that is impossible.' The cool tones were unmistakably Wolf's. So was the authoritative indifference to her feelings. The *bastard*.

'You're inhuman!' Her voice broke on surging anger as she hurled the words at the grille. 'Whoever you are, whatever you think you're achieving, you're just vicious scum! God above, do you even bother to think what this is going to do to my father?'

'Look beside the mattress,' the disembodied voice instructed, as though she hadn't even spoken. 'The airways bag contains several things you are going to need. Open it now.'

'Go to hell!' she snapped, raking her ruined hair back from her forehead.

'Open it.'

'Damn you,' she whispered, snatching the bag closer. The sense of frustration, of being totally controlled, was almost unbearable. Ever since this man had materialised in front of her in the study, she'd been as utterly in his command as a mouse in the claws of a cat. She was grinding her teeth as she yanked the zip of the bag open.

'Use the torch sparingly,' Wolf went on in the same level tone. 'It will give only four or five hours' light. There is some fresh fruit in the packet, and black coffee in the flask. Be sparing with these also.' She dug beneath the things he'd mentioned to find the real treasure in the bag—a small transistor radio. Joy actually made her grin as she clutched it. That, more than anything, would make the dark hours bearable. 'There are replacement batteries for the radio in the bag.' Wolf paused. 'It will be some hours before you can come out. Be patient. Nothing you can do in there can be heard from the outside—so don't waste nervous energy screaming or banging. You understand?'

She didn't reply.

'I'm putting out the lights now. They will not go on again. Nor will I use the internal communication system. That is not for the sake of cruelty, Miss Cheyne, merely an essential security measure.'

'Please,' she asked suddenly. 'Magda—the housekeeper—is she hurt?'

'Your servant was unharmed,' he replied coolly.

'I simply tied her up. By now she will be free. Rest now. You've been through a lot.'

As the lights clicked off, Susie grabbed for the torch, and flicked on its comforting beam to fight down her nerves. The pseudo-concern in the cool voice didn't fool her for a second. She had never hated anyone in her whole life the way she hated Comrade Wolf. What was he, a German? The quiet accent was impeccable, cultured, the voice of a radio announcer. Too perfect, perhaps, to be that of an Englishman. *'Miss Cheyne'*—the urbane politeness was as disgusting as the mocking concern for her welfare. She'd already experienced too much of the destructive male energy that lay beneath the polished veneer to be lulled by it now.

She had hardly had a chance to look at his face; she dredged in her shifting memories for an image of a ruthless jawline, clear tiger's eyes that were made frightening by the level line of harsh black eyebrows. The hair had been close-cropped, though she seemed to remember flecks of grey at the dark temples.

The face of a killer, a kidnapper, an executive in the world of organised violence. Thirty? Thirty-five? It was Wolf who was evidently the commander of the group, Wolf who was now driving her—to she knew not where. An image of an anonymous body, riddled with bullet-holes, rose starkly in her mind's eye. Was that how she herself would eventually be found, maybe weeks or months from now?

The thought of her father's horror was agony to her. The kidnappers were going to demand a massive ransom for her, that was certain. How was her father going to react? She knew he'd do everything in his power to keep her from harm, to the extent of destroying his own empire, if needs be. Would he try to handle it on his own? Would he bring in the police? He'd have little choice about that, she realised. This was a terrorist incident. Police business. Chillingly, the phrase rolled through her mind. *A terrorist incident.* Somehow, she and her father had been caught up in the undercover war that raged between the police and terrorists all over Europe, and God alone knew what was going to become of them both.

Restlessly, she swung the torch's beam on to the mattress, and hunted for the radio. Her fear was something she simply had to control if she was to keep her nerves from jumping out of her skin.

Mustering her courage, she switched off the torch, and fiddled with the dial of the little radio. She found a soothing music station with regular newsflashes, and curled up with the tiny, yet somehow wonderfully reassuring sound. She'd be able to hear, at least, when the news of her capture broke, as it surely would. Maybe even hear her father's voice on the radio.

The thought of him wrenched her heartstrings, bringing wetness to her eyes again. He was going to have to go through so much, an agony that would strain his poised exterior to the uttermost limits, tearing at his emotions. He was going to suffer more than she herself ever possibly could. Physical brutality was easier to bear than the silent torture of waiting.

And now that her mother was dead, she was all that was left of his family. The kidnappers must have chosen her so carefully, such a very soft target. The cruelty of what was being done hit her afresh, in a new wave of hatred for the people who could conceive of and execute a crime as callous as blackmail. Poor Dad, poor, poor man. For the first time ever, Susie felt relief that her mother wasn't alive. Alive to go through this. . . .

The vibrating darkness swelled around her as the minutes blurred into an hour, two hours, the noise of the engine sometimes drowning the tinny music on the radio. She ate a peach and drank some of the bitter coffee, then slept for what felt like another hour, and woke feeling horribly nervy and confused, longing for sleep again. It came unexpectedly, obliterating the raw sinews and stretched nerves of her mind.

The truck was stopped when she woke again, though the engine was still running. A border-post, perhaps, or just a filling-station. Half-heartedly, she considered screaming, then shrugged the useless idea off. Better, as Comrade Wolf had suggested, to save her energy. She wondered idly where she was being taken. Down to Italy? There would certainly be plenty of terrorist contacts there. Or to Germany? She searched for the names of the urban guerilla groups that had been written so bloodily in the headlines over the past decade, and couldn't find them. She felt the gears engage, and then they were moving off again, the packing-cases shifting slightly as the truck angled downhill, and the roaring darkness made coherent thought almost impossible. But she was growing certain that a political group was responsible for the kidnapping, not simple criminals. Both Senta and the brutal driver had mouthed the inane slogans of violent radicalism, the bitter denunciations which were so much a part of the ultra-Left or ultra-Right factions.

That realisation also chilled her. There was

always an underlying streak of insanity in political kidnappings. How many victims there had been who had never left their captors' clutches alive—the gentle Italian ex-President, the German industrialist. . . .

She shut the thoughts away, back in the dark dungeons of her brain where they'd slithered from. The idea of escape stirred restlessly inside her. Maybe there would be a chance, just maybe. . . .

The long hours were making her desperate, her nerves fraying badly, when the movement ceased for a second time. And then the engines ground to a halt. The silence seemed to roar even louder than the motors for a long while, and Susie sat up nervously, hugging the blankets to her chin.

The clashing of the bolts on the tail-gate had her staggering to her feet—and then the doors swung open wide. It was night, and the cool rush of fresh air was infinitely delicious. She ran to the ramp, her legs feeling weak. Wolf was waiting, a tall, dark figure in jeans and a black leather jacket. The night sky was deep, shimmering with stars, and as she clambered out, she saw that the truck was parked on a deserted mountain road, among a vast forest of pines.

His fingers bit into her arm as he helped her down.

'How do you feel?'

'Wretched,' she snapped, snatching her arm away. 'Don't touch me. Where are we?'

'Here,' he said calmly.

'Big secret,' she sneered. The place could have been anywhere in Switzerland. Or anywhere in Italy, Germany, even Austria or France. But the summer night was wonderful after her captivity! She turned her back on him, not wanting to have him in her view, and stretched luxuriously, reaching up to the silvery half-moon above. The pines murmured in the breeze, and their cleansing scent hung sweetly on the air.

'At the bottom of this bank is a small stream,' he said, watching her with unreadable eyes. 'You will be private there.'

She glanced down the bank, and turned to him with a twisted smile.

'You mean you trust me that far?'

'There's nowhere for you to run to,' he answered indifferently. 'It wouldn't take me long to find you if you tried.'

Loathing his sureness, Susie scrambled down the slope to where the little river glinted among the tall pines. Their dead needles made a soft carpet under her bare feet. The rustle of the stream was soothing on her jarred nerves. Once out of sight of the road, she made a hurried toilet as best she could. The water was icy as she rinsed her face, and pressed her hands against the pebbly bottom, wishing the water could rinse away memory, too.

How lovely this would be—under any other circumstances. She had to force herself to walk back up the slope to the truck. Revulsion flooded her at the thought of being with Wolf again, of having to enter that noisy jail full of chocolate boxes. Her feet felt like lead as she dragged them back towards her horrible mobile prison.

He was sitting in the cab as she stepped on to the road, the light glowing softly above him. He swung the door open for her.

'Come up here.'

'No thank you,' she gritted. She wanted to stay outside in the air—and there was always the chance that someone would drive past, someone she could signal to——

'Come.'

The command in his voice was a rock that broke the uneven line of her will. Silently, she clambered up into the cab beside him. There wasn't any sense in inviting force if it wasn't necessary. Wrily, she realised she was learning a hard lesson with these people. A lesson of survival. He took her chin in hard fingers, and tilted her face to the light.

'Are you all right in the back?'

Narrowing her eyes against the dazzle, she tried to twist her face away.

'I'm all right. Let me go.'

'You look pale.' He released her chin, and laid cool knuckles against her forehead. 'And you're hot.'

'What the hell did you expect, for God's sake?' she retorted, her voice shaky with rising emotion. She glared at him, wishing she had a man's strength to lash out at him. The overhead light emphasised the hawklike cast of his face, pooling shadows under his cheeks and in the curve of his lips. 'What you've been doing to me these past hours hasn't exactly been calculated to make me feel well, has it?'

'No.' There was no emotion in the monosyllable. He reached up and switched off the light. Through the tinted windscreen, the moonlight lit the interior of the cab softly.

He didn't feel a damned thing for her, not even a pang of remorse for her feelings. She stared out at the pine-flanked road ahead. 'When exactly are you going to contact my father?' she asked. The question had been meant to sound even, cool. It came out trembling, the tears in it very audible.

'It would be better for your own sake if you knew nothing, Miss Cheyne.'

'Damn you,' she quavered, the tears very close now, 'can't you for once show a shred of—of humanity——'

His arm came round her shoulder. She tried fiercely to shake it away, but treacherous weakness brought the choking sobs to her throat, making her gulp helplessly. He drew her tight against him as she gave way to racking, dry sobs that seemed to twist her very heart and soul. His warmth was paradoxically comforting, reinforcing the temporary make-believe that the formidable strength in his body was a protection, not a threat.

For a bare minute. She drew away from him, revolted by her own weakness, and slid across the seat to the other end of the cab, as far from him as possible.

'What you're doing is the most despicable thing in the world,' she said in a low voice, wiping her eyes. She felt bruised inside, repelled by a world that was more sinister and vicious than she'd ever dreamed. 'Tormenting an innocent man to get money out of him, abusing a father's love——'

'Why assume that your father is our target?' He prised open a plastic box, and passed it to her. The simple cold chicken salad in it nauseated her.

'If you're thinking of trying to extort money out of Chemical Suisse,' she retorted with a bitter little laugh, 'you're in for a nasty shock. Those people wouldn't part with a penny to save their grandmothers. And you can tell that to your so-called Executive Committee.' She pushed the box away. 'No thank you, I'm not hungry.'

'I don't care whether you're hungry or not,' he said sharply. 'You need food. Now eat it.'

Under that level stare, she took the box sullenly, and picked at the food with her fingers. Once again, she thought wrily, these people were showing themselves masters of camouflage; the man beside her, in his rough, used clothes, was the perfect image of a big truck-driver. Even if someone were to drive by on this lonely road, all they would see would be a trucker and his blonde, cheap-looking girlfriend eating a snack among the pines.

'I want you to listen carefully, Miss Cheyne,' he said softly, leaning on the wide steering-wheel to study her with hooded eyes. 'Because this is important to your continued well-being.'

'Oh, sure!' she snorted, her mouth full of the chicken, which was unexpectedly delicious, 'you're all fired-up about my well-being, aren't you— Comrade Wolf?'

'The organisation which now controls your fate,' he went on, ignoring her interruption, 'doesn't play games. Please don't make the mistake of thinking we're eccentric amateurs— we're not. There are people in my organisation whose ruthlessness would appall you. If you had even the slightest inkling of the things that could happen to you, and have happened to others before you, your young bones would freeze inside you.' She gnawed at the chicken, silenced by the calm authority in his words. 'Compared to some of my colleagues, Miss Cheyne, I am a benevolent Father Christmas. And you know what I can do.'

'I've had ample evidence,' she agreed bitterly. She wiped her mouth, trying not to show him that she'd been impressed by what he'd said. She wasn't inclined to accept his control, but every minute spent in the cab staved off her return to the prison behind. 'So?'

'I want you to believe me whan I say that any chance you have of getting out of this alive——' his mouth tightened '—and unmutilated—lies with me.'

'My hero.' But her gaze had been unwillingly dragged to his eyes, glinting emerald-silver in the dim light. To this man, her façade of schoolgirl bravado was probably as substantial as tissue-paper.

'For your own sake,' he said, and there was almost a note of urgency in the quiet voice, 'do exactly as I say, always. If you disobey me at any time or in any of the places where we have to go, you will be merely endangering your own life. And if you attempt to escape, I will no longer be able to protect you. Stay close to me. Do you under-stand?'

She stared at him, licking her fingers in doubt. There was something so compelling about him, something so authoritative in the way he spoke. Or was that just her gut reaction to the fact that he was a lethally handsome man? And how in the name of God could she give her confidence to someone who was almost certainly a trained killer?

'Sure,' she said glibly, covering her inner confusion with a shrug as she turned away. 'You seem slightly less crazy than your colleagues, I admit.' She didn't add that of all of them, it was he who frightened her most, and whom she was most sure could kill without compunction. Yet perhaps he had been given some order to keep her unharmed, some directive from the shadowy Executive Committee, whoever they were. Maybe in that her safety lay. 'Who are you, anyway? I mean, all of you—some kind of terror squad?'

'Our aim is not terror,' he replied sharply. 'Simply social justice.'

'What,' she retorted, 'by breaking the law?'

'Laws are made by the rich to keep the poor subjugated.' He took the now-empty box from her, and dropped it into a bag behind his seat. 'What you call "law" is simply organised tyranny.'

'Nonsense,' she gasped, almost amused by his cool illogicality. 'The laws are made by the people——'

'Rich, strong people. Like you and your kind.' His eyes raked hers. 'Society must be smashed to pieces so that it can be rebuilt. Operations like this one help us raise the money needed for that great task.'

'For Heaven's sake,' Susie exclaimed, 'what makes you think society *wants* to be rebuilt?'

'No doubt life seems very pleasant from your sheltered eyrie,' he said levelly. 'Instead of studying the plants and little fishes in such careful detail, perhaps you should have spared a minute to see how your fellow-humans were faring. Perhaps then you would have noticed that the industrial society destroys men and women and their defenceless children—not just weeds and molluscs.'

'I'm as aware of inequality as you are,' she retorted. This was the kind of argument she'd heard going on in university refectories, and it didn't impress her. 'That doesn't justify what you and your gangsters do to the same innocent people—Oh, what's the use?' She ran her fingers in frustration through her cropped hair. 'Men of violence like you won't listen to reason. It's been proved all over the world.' She turned to him, acid lines etched round her mouth and eyes. 'All your political jargon is just a cover, isn't it, Comrade

Wolf? Marx means less to you than the pleasure of inflicting pain and terror on the helpless. You do this because you want to. Because you like it.'

'Society is at war,' he said softly. He zipped the front of his jacket up. 'It's been at war for a long time, and people like you are only beginning to find out the truth. We will win in the end, Miss Cheyne, I assure you.'

'Don't count on it,' she retorted. 'The world's too full of good people. People like Joe.' She winced inwardly, though, at the thought of quiet, intellectual Joe meeting the lethal edge of Comrade Wolf.

He glanced at his watch. 'It's time to be on the road again.'

Susie stiffened, the prospect of going back into her prison rising like a nightmare in front of her. As if catching the movement, Wolf glanced across at her.

'War makes the rules.' His voice was gentle. 'Not us.'

'I hate it in there,' she said unsteadily, twisting her fingers together. 'I—I'm afraid of the dark. I have been, ever since I was a child. Please——' She reached out to touch his arm. 'Let me stay here while you drive—if only for a few minutes——'

'You know that's impossible,' he said quietly.

'I'll be good, I give you my word!'

'And by and by some crazy scheme will get into your stupid head,' he said with an ironic smile, 'and you'll try and knock me on the skull. And then I'd be forced to hurt you.'

She bit her lip hard, fighting down the depression and anger that engulfed her as he climbed out of the cab, and came round to swing her door open. He lifted her down, the steely strength of his arms making her eight stone seem even lighter than it was. She thrust herself out of his hands, feeling as though his touch would defile her, and stalked off in front of him, regretting ever having shown him any weakness. Had she forgotten that he was the sort of man whose enjoyment would simply be heightened by seeing her suffer?

She took a last, hungry look at the whispering pines and the moonlit sky as he swung open the tail-gate, drinking the cool air into her lungs.

'You've been courageous so far, Miss Cheyne.' He helped her up the ramp, the metal cold under her bare feet. 'Be courageous for another few hours.'

'Go to hell,' she muttered. The faint smell of chocolates greeted her sickeningly. Her last sight, before he swung the steel doors closed, and bolted them from the outside, was of the moonlight glistening in those enigmatic, cool eyes.

She crawled to her mattress, and groped for blankets as the engines started up beneath her.

She felt profoundly depressed now. The initial shock of the kidnapping had worn off, and the adrenalin which had helped keep her spirits high had long since been reabsorbed. Her kidnappers were political fanatics. Even Wolf, the most mature of them all, spouted the meaningless slogans of the far Left. Her chances of coming out of this alive now seemed impossibly slight to her. And the thought of her father's agony made it infinitely worse. He would be awake now, she knew, sitting tautly by the telephone, waiting for news, anything that would tell him whether his daughter was alive or dead. What impossible sum were the terrorists going to demand for her release? Something that would break him financially for ever?

That cold, calculating bastard up front—damn his green eyes! She ground her teeth in helpless hatred of the cruelty which had pervaded this whole operation. And Comrade Wolf was the most cruel and calculating of all. Even Senta, with the pale sadistic light in her eyes, was almost pitiable, a twisted personality. But he, with that smooth voice, the polished veneer of breeding, was the most vicious of all.

She fumbled for the radio, and flipped it on. The jumble of stations, French, German and Italian, told her nothing about her location, but she found some peaceful night-music, and rolled on to her back, trying to chase her blues away with some sweet memory.

And little had been sweeter than that last summer in Nova Scotia. She'd felt so free, as though her spirit had broken loose from fetters. At last she was getting over the cloud that had followed her mother's death, and was putting her own life together. And, too, she was getting used to her job, learning how to put into practice all the knowledge she'd crammed into her head during three years at university.

The job had come through the International Geophysical Committee, a mandate to study the effect of pollution on several key coastal sites where effluents of various kinds washed out into the ocean from inland industries. For three months she had followed the peninsular's majestic coastline from end to end, sometimes liaising with Oceanographic Survey colleagues, sometimes staying with research people, but most often camping on beaches in a tent or in the VW minibus the

Canadians had given her. Alone, under the sometimes awesome skies, always within sight of the rolling grey majesty of the Atlantic.

And looking back, she could see that although constrained by the discipline of her job and the meticulous routine of samples and tests, she'd more or less let herself run wild. Over those three months her hair had become a dark, rich tangle, her skin gilded by the fierce sun, then burned almost to mahogany, so that with the exception of her storm-blue eyes, Susan Cheyne might have been some Mohican princess wandering along the jagged shoreline. Switzerland and England had been tiny compared to the vastness of Canada. The scale of Canada had helped to lift her heart, make it soar. She'd been twenty-one, a supremely healthy young adult testing her wings after the limitations of school and university.

And her stunning good looks and slender grace had brought her suitors wherever she went. Tanned young Adonises from the cities who played football and tennis like pros, and regarded her test-tubes and meters with indulgent patronage. Or bearded and earnest scientists, eager to discuss their work. Or cocky, dark-skinned boys from the fishing-towns, whose aggressive, abrasive ways had been sometimes charming, sometimes a little frightening. A consensus of masculine admiration from north to south that would have made a less mature woman drunk on vanity and self-confidence.

A smile crept across the bruised satin of her lips. Compared with the Canadians of last summer, Englishmen were diffident and shy. This summer, though, had been different. Maybe as lovely in its way; but without the vast grandeur of Nova

Scotia. The Marine Studies group had offered her
a similar research job at the beginning of the year,
studying the effect that nuclear power-stations
were having on marine life. She'd accepted with
alacrity, finding the challenge a fascinating one;
the question was not one of radiation, as she'd at
first supposed, but of the hot water which was
pumped out into the sea from the generators'
cooling systems. In at least one place she'd been
amazed to find an almost sub-tropical colony
flourishing around the outlet of an electricity-
generating station.

And again, she'd been camping on the beaches,
or sleeping in the back of her Land Rover, waking
to glowing dawns and drinking in sunlit days.
There hadn't been nearly as many suntanned
Adonises, though! Except for Joe. Not that he was
an Adonis, exactly; but with that shy smile and
those heart-meltingly soulful eyes, Joe Dowson
was distinctly attractive. Dr Joseph Dowson, PhD,
head of the marine research station of Fairbourne,
where they'd met, and enjoyed a highly technical
discussion about salinity levels. Warmth had
passed between them, laughter and smiles that
weren't just part of the work they shared, but grew
from an instantaneous, maybe even a deep,
magnetism. They'd seen a lot more of each other
over the next fortnight.

The night before she'd left for Switzerland to
stay with her father for three weeks, he'd taken her
to the most expensive restaurant in the area.
Afterwards, in his venerable but immaculate MG,
they'd talked lazily and contentedly under a full
moon. And had ended by kissing passionately,
both left with beating hearts and wide eyes by the
force of their mutual attraction.

She smiled again, rolling over dreamily. They'd made no commitments on the eve of her departure—but they'd both known instinctively that this would be waiting for them when she returned. This happy, exciting relationship, more serious in its implications than anything she'd yet experienced—theirs to take where they wanted.

Life had been very good to her. It had given her a job that thousands would have envied, a job that took her into the open air almost every day, gave her discretion to work with minimal supervision, introduced her to fascinating, valuable people, people like Joe Dowson. As for politics, at least violent politics, they'd never even touched her existence until fourteen or sixteen hours ago, when this horror had struck at her from a cloudless sky.

The remembrance of where she was descended on her, darker than the pitch blackness all around. Suddenly, she sat up, and turned the radio's volume louder. The music had given way to a news report, read in Italian. Biting her lip, she struggled to decipher the too-rapid monologue.

Her disappearance was high up among the important news items; the story seemed to have broken late in the evening, after a news conference given by the Zurich police. The announcer's unemotional voice appealed for information, gave a description of how she'd last been dressed.

'The Swiss police have issued a recent photograph, and are asking the public to be on the alert. Susan Cheyne is 162 cm tall, has long black hair and blue eyes, and when last seen was wearing a white cotton summer dress and carrying a black shoulderbag. . . .'

She winced. Even if someone by some chance

were to catch a glimpse of her, she couldn't possibly be associated with that description now. Also, continued the newsreader, it was thought that a green Fiat seen near the house that morning might be connected with the kidnappers. It had had a Spanish numberplate.

'Chief among the groups suspected of the abduction,' the tinny voice concluded, 'are the recently formed Alba Rossa, generally regarded by the authorities as among the most dangerous of the successors to the notorious Red Brigades, whose organisation was uncovered by Milan police three years ago. No ransom, however, has yet been demanded.

'At the summit meeting in Paris, the German premier warned Common Market members. . . .'

Susie heard the newscast out, waiting for the newsreader to sign off. He did so, announcing that the station was called *Radio Piemontana*. Radio Piedmont? Did that mean they were in Piedmont, heading for the coast, or the Alpes Maritimes? Useless to speculate, but at least she had some idea that she was in northern Italy, maybe fairly near Torino or Milan. She switched the radio off, her heart beating faster. It was a weird feeling to hear her kidnapping described on a radio news service. Would the story make the British media? Would her friends, maybe even Joe, be listening with horror to the same news?

It was also frustrating in the extreme to realise how far the police, with their green Fiats and white dresses, were from the facts. How damnably clever her captors were being.

Alba Rossa? That meant Red Dawn. She pulled a wry face. What an optimistic, melodramatic name for a gang of fanatical thugs.

She pulled the blanket over her shoulders, and lay in the darkness, thinking of her father.

CHAPTER FOUR

WHEN next the tail-gate was thrown open, daylight flooded into the truck, blinding Susie as she rose, half-asleep, on unsteady legs.

'Wh-where are we?'

'At our destination.' Wolf took her arm, guiding her outside. She squeezed her eyes shut as the painful sunlight hit her, hot and brilliant. Her bare feet stumbled on grass, but she jerked her arm away from him, and forced herself to look about herself. It was a magnificent day. The countryside all around was wild and hilly, and totally deserted except for the farmhouse they had arrived at. The burnt-orange tiles on the square building, and the massive Lombardy pines that grew all around, suggested Italy. Two men dressed in rough peasant clothes were waiting for them, one carrying a shotgun in the crook of his arm. But she didn't have much chance to assess her surroundings before someone twisted her arm into a painful grip, and hustled her rapidly to the house. She turned to throw a glance back helplessly at Wolf. He wasn't even looking. And the truck, which had formerly borne the Motta logo, now had a sign reading *Di Bari, Prodotti Agricolturali*. Quick-change artist, she thought wrily. And then she was being pushed through the door into the gloom of a provincial farmhouse.

'Hello, *liebchen*.'

Susie's heart sank. She must have taken another route to be here to meet them. Like the men, Senta was wearing peasant dress, and a coarse scarf that covered her blonde hair. But the automatic in her hand was black and shiny. She pointed to one wall.

'Over there.' She followed as the men walked Susie to the lone chair against the blank wall. 'So—you had a good trip, little *bourgeoise*?'

'Not bad,' Susie retorted. Some vindictive female instinct, prompted by the memory of Senta leaning up to kiss Wolf yesterday, made her add, 'Wolf made me *very* comfortable, thank you.' Anger flared in the other woman's eyes, and she stepped forward to slap at Susie's unprotected face, hard. The blow glanced accidentally off one of the men's arms, catching Susie on the jaw. Then she was being forced into the chair.

So, she thought, her heart pounding, there was a raw place in Senta's armoury, connected with Comrade Wolf! Had she tried to court his favours, and been rebuffed? Wolf's indifferent pose yesterday had certainly hinted at that. *That* was something to remember, too! Any sign of weakness in this team was worth remembering.

The heavier of the men had produced a black wig, not unlike the style that Susie had worn her own hair in before her forced cut the day before. She sat bewildered as they fitted it on to her head, wondering what new madness was being planned.

'Hang the flag up behind her,' Senta ordered. She was obviously in command of the men, and the hatred in her light-blue eyes boded ill for Susie's future comfort. The flag they hung on the wall behind was hand-painted on a calico sheet. It showed a large red star in which was a black hammer and sickle. The crude letters above read, *'Alba Rossa—La Lotta Continue'*. Susie had to bite back her grimace. 'The struggle goes on.' The struggle against whom? Innocent people, like her and her father?

Senta crouched quickly with the Polaroid camera, and the blue flashcube popped. She collected the emerging photograph with a cotton handkerchief, careful not to touch it with her bare skin, and showed it to Susie with a sneer.

'Beautiful, eh *liebchen*?'

Susie's own face stared back at her, pale and tired against the garish flag. There was no hint of any other background, and the grainy quality of the print made the wig look exactly like her own hair. No one would suspect that she was now a cropped blonde. And the shot had been cut off at her neck, so that her clothing was invisible.

Very clever.

The taller 'peasant' jerked her to her feet roughly. He was overweight, his heavy jowls covered in a three- or four-days' stubble. A thick nose spread from under brutal, lowering brows. The heavy belly, though, concealed a formidable strength, and Susie staggered as he pushed her casually towards the next room.

'*Avanti,*' he grunted. She heard Senta's malicious laugh as the brutish man jerked her towards a set of narrow stairs leading down to what must be a cellar.

'Perhaps Draco will make you very comfortable too—eh, *liebchen*? He is our host, after all.'

The thought of another dark, confined prison appalled Susie as she stumbled down the dank stairs. And her worst fears were confirmed by the cellar beneath. It was damp, and smelled unpleasantly of mould and wet-rot, and the single 40-watt bulb did nothing to enhance these charms.

The man called Draco pushed her through the barrels and empty crates that filled the cellar. She caught a rank smell of manure and unwashed flesh from his rough clothes. Through her fear, Susie realised that Draco was essentially different from the rest of the team—probably the master of this place, a half-idiot peasant who had been bribed or gulled into becoming the accomplice of the terrorists.

At the other end of the cellar a low doorway had been cleverly concealed behind an old-fashioned boiler. Draco made no attempt to fit his bulk through the narrow gap. He thrust Susie past the thankfully cool boiler, and sent her staggering into the little, shadowy room beyond. Then he slammed the door shut, and locked it, and she could faintly hear him dragging something heavy across the door to conceal it. Then only a deep silence.

She sank on to the bare floor, her throat locking in a silent sob, pressing the heels of her hands into her eyes. The bag, with the precious torch and radio, were still in the truck. She fought the tears back fiercely, trying to control the fear that threatened to dominate her. She had never felt so utterly lost, so utterly threatened. She was completely at the mercy of the people who had kidnapped her, defenceless against whatever they chose to do to her in the name of some crazed justice, or out of sheer sadism. She had no idea where she was, or whether she would ever leave this place alive.

She opened her eyes slowly. Even if she were to scream, no one would hear. The walls of the little cell had been lined with grey soundproof tiles. There was no window. The door had neither keyhole nor handle, but had been tiled like the walls.

She picked herself up, and sat down on the low bunk-bed that was the only piece of furniture in the room. From somewhere inside, she dredged at strength. She was going to need it. In the corner were a plastic jug and a plastic basin. The weak bulb overhead was protected by a stout wire grille. To stop her from using it to cut her own wrists, no doubt. How horrible, how very horrible, to even conceive of locking a human being in a place like this.

'Bastards,' she whispered, shaking her head in tired horror. 'Cruel, inhuman, bastards. . . .'

At least, though, if they had taken her photograph, some kind of ransom demand might be made shortly. With luck, with a great deal of luck, her ordeal might not last long.

Something was pricking her thigh through the pocket of her jeans. Dully, she fished it out. It was the cross which Wolf had given back to her at Zurich. She pressed the little sliver of gold to her lips, deeply grateful to have something to hold on to, no matter how tiny.

She sat up with a start as the bolts on the door were unfastened. She'd been standing on the cliffs at Cape Sable, staring out over the brooding majesty of the rocks below, the surging grey Atlantic far beneath. . . . The last shreds of her dream drifted away, leaving her with the dreary knowledge of her reality. It was Wolf who pushed the door open, carrying a tray. She looked away from the tall, tanned figure, her mouth twisted with dislike, and ran her hands through her short, bleached hair. It felt stiff and dirty.

'I've brought you some food,' he said, laying the tray on the bed beside her. She looked at the bowl of spaghetti in a rich tomato sauce. One of her favourite meals—she'd practically lived on spaghetti in Canada. Hunger dragged at her empty stomach, weakening her pride. 'Eat,' he said gently, as though anticipating her refusal. 'You must be starving.'

He closed the door as she picked the bowl up unwillingly, and turned to watch her eat. He had changed from his truck-drivers' outfit into black denims that hugged his lean hips and a black cotton T-shirt. The simple clothes emphasised the honed fitness of his body, and with a stab of envy she reflected that he looked clean and refreshed. She herself was feeling creased, grubby—and to think she'd been jibbing at the thought of having her hair done and her nails varnished!

'I feel a mess,' she complained as she quickly ate the crude satisfaction of the pasta. She looked up resentfully into his tanned face. 'Can't I have a bath?'

'No.'

'No,' she repeated acidly. 'Just like that. The law according to Comrade Wolf.' She scooped up a forkful of the delicious spaghetti. 'Is it absolutely necessary that I stay filthy?'

'You are a very impatient young woman, Miss Cheyne.'

Susie snorted, irritated by his polite manner. 'Please—let's cut out this "Miss Cheyne" stuff—*Comrade* Wolf.'

'Okay.' He ignored her sneer. 'Susan. You could have a bath if you insist. It so happens that Draco is on duty tonight. You've already met Draco? Well, he would have to accompany you to the bathroom, and make sure you behaved yourself.' He smiled slightly at her expression. 'Comrade Draco is—how shall I describe it? An impulsive person. It might be better to wait until Senta comes on duty.'

'There's not much to choose between any of you,' Susie said sulkily, returning to her pasta. The thought of Draco's hot animal eyes on her naked body had effectively demolished all her desire to bathe. There was a stone jug of wine on the tray, and Wolf poured a glassful for her, then sat on the other end of the bed, resting his arms on one drawn-up knee.

'You can bath tomorrow,' he said. She put down her empty plate, gulped down a mouthful of the harsh country wine, and leaned back to study him properly for the first time.

Her initial impression of icy authority was confirmed. And there was a lot more.

He was quite devastatingly handsome in a fiercely masculine way. The combination of those shockingly direct green eyes and that subtle, carved mouth made for one of the most intriguing male faces she'd ever seen. It cut her to the quick to acknowledge it, but Comrade Wolf was physically the most beautiful man she'd come across in her twenty-two years. Beautiful, cruel, and challenging.

Level black brows and thick eyelashes emphasised the shock of that emerald-green gaze, so startlingly cool against the golden skin; and there was a sensuous line to the deeply chiselled lips that promised a passionate, humorous nature. Something which hadn't materialised so far, she thought sardonically. His face was lean, a formidable strength evident in the set of his jaw, and his dark hair was cropped close at his temples, but not too close to hide the silver flecks that invited her to put his age at thirty-five. Mature, and very, very deadly. The tanned arms were powerful. No watch or rings. The black cotton shirt clung to the sleek shape of muscles that had obviously been tempered by relentless hours and years of exercise. What, she puzzled—swimming? The taut poise of his whole body suggested something more aggressive. Fencing?

Of course, she thought, suddenly ashamed of finding him so desirable. Excuse me, Comrade Wolf, for missing the exercise you enjoy most of all. Killing people.

His eyes met hers, and Susie dropped her gaze, feeling her throat and cheeks flushing.

'Why aren't you all going around in hoods or something?' she demanded. 'Aren't you afraid I'll identify you when you eventually let me go?' She forced a laugh. 'Or aren't you planning to let me go?'

'We are fighters,' he said calmly. 'Not criminals. We do not hide our faces.'

'Extortion is a crime,' she snapped back.

'Nothing is a crime when it is committed in the name of the revolution,' he returned. Speechless, Susie could only shake her head. Did he *really* believe what he was saying? 'Alba Rossa speaks and acts for the paralysed proletariat, broken in spirit and will by the masters who exploit them.'

'What—do you think you'd get a single ordinary working man or woman out there to applaud your actions?' Susie demanded angrily. 'You must be crazy!'

'If it were not for the support of ordinary working men and women, we would not be able to

function at all.' The cool statement silenced her. A
faint smile touched his eyes, but not his mouth.
'There are many who dream of the red dawn to
come, Susan. Very many indeed.'

'The ones you've managed to poison,' Susie
gritted, thinking of the far-Left contingent she
occasionally met through her research work.
They'd been a singularly unimpressive lot. 'All the
loonies, the twisted minds, the weirdos. And the
trendy young radicals who applaud you while not
having the faintest idea what you *really* do and
what you're *really* like!'

'Bravo.' He clapped sardonically. 'So you have a
political thought in your head, after all.'

'I detest violence,' she told him angrily, looking
away from the beautiful green eyes. 'That's not a
political opinion—it's just common humanity. I'm
a scientist, not some kind of capitalist monster.'

'Ah, yes,' he purred, 'a scientist. "All the
evidence points to an increasing level of mercury
and other heavy-metal toxins at or around the
mouths of rivers and estuaries."'

She looked up in astonishment. He had just
quoted from her report to the Canadian
Government last year.

'You seem to know a lot about me,' she said
warily. The cool scientific language had sounded
odd on his lips—somehow suiting him much better
than the Marxist jargon!

'We study each project we undertake with
considerable care.' There was a glint almost of
mockery in the cool eyes. 'It's important to make
sure the groundwork is completely accurate. I
quite enjoyed your report, as a matter of fact.'

'There,' Susie retorted acidly, 'and I was
thinking you were just a bunch of vicious thugs.'

'Our predecessors were clumsy.' Wolf's eyes studied the tense line of her body calmly as she turned away in disgust. 'The Red Brigades, Baader-Meinhof—dangerous, but crude. They were all caught. We will not be. Alba Rossa is a new generation, Susan, with new ways and new skills. A great deal of research and planning went into this operation.'

'Why me, then?' she demanded bitterly. 'What the hell have my father or I ever done?'

'You were a perfect target,' he replied, eyebrows arching in surprise. 'Can't you see that? In the first place, you are beautiful.' She winced, hating the unemotional way the compliment had been delivered. 'And beauty means extra publicity. Then, too, your mother is dead, and you are an only child.' Wolf smiled icily. 'Details which will make doubly sure that your father is—shall I say, co-operative?'

Blinding fury made her claw at his face, her teeth bared. He caught her wrists easily, and imprisoned them in a grip like velvet steel. She struggled madly for a few seconds, then slumped back in sick anger.

'You're a monster,' she said, staring into the amused eyes.

'I'm a professional,' he corrected. He released her wrists, his fingers leaving white weals against the tanned skin. 'There were other reasons why you were chosen,' he went on, as she rubbed her wrists. 'Your connection with Chemical Suisse, for example. Chemical Suisse happens to be one of the most powerful elements in the military-industrial complex. It pours money into capitalist coffers, puts bullets into the guns of capitalist soldiers. By hitting Chemical Suisse, we hit the Western power-structure in its weakest place—its pocket-book.' A passionate glint lit his eyes. 'Be proud, Susan Cheyne—indirectly, you are helping to hasten the collapse of the decadent old order. And the rise of the new.'

He rose, and looked down at Susie. 'One other thing. Maybe I'm a monster to you. I don't expect you to understand me or the reason I fight. But remember what I told you in the truck, Susan. Your only hope of safety lies with me. Don't do anything, don't ask for anything, unless I'm there. Remember that.' He didn't wait for an answer. She sat in rigid silence as he took her glass, and put her plate back on to the tray. The brush of his knuckles against her hair was almost too light to be called a caress, but it made her flinch nonetheless. 'Be brave, little scientist,' he said gently.

And she heard the door close behind him.

She let her pent-up breath out explosively. What an extraordinary man he was, moving from icy fanaticism to almost kindly gentleness in a second. Maybe that was the psychological profile which a terrorist had to have—an almost schizophrenic split between emotion and intellect. He still frightened her, more than ever. There was a formidable strength about Comrade Wolf which had nothing to do with his trained muscles.

'For God's sake, Susie,' she whispered to herself, 'don't ever underestimate him, no matter how physically charming he may be.'

The whispered words made no echo in the soundproofed room. But they left her with narrowed, thoughtful eyes. It was the first time she'd confessed to herself that Wolf was an attractive man. Maybe that confession was even more dangerous than the guns of Alba Rossa. Wolf's attractiveness was as potentially devastating as a sub-machine-gun. And perhaps 'attraction' was the wrong word; it was a quality which didn't just tug at her emotions, but which lashed out at her senses, dominating them, attacking them.

She closed her eyes, biting her lip. She felt almost unbearably uncomfortable, her body grimy and unwashed, the shabby jeans far too tight for comfort, her nerves stretched to snapping-point.

Boredom was going to be a killer.

Boredom in which her fear could gnaw at her courage. Boredom in which that potent fascination with Wolf could grow irrationally. Her mind twisted away from the memory of that powerful male body, the way the muscles of his flanks and stomach had moulded the black cotton. She needed comfort now, ached for a reassuring male presence—and that made Wolf doubly magnetic.

Damn.

She stood up and kicked off her jeans, sighing with relief as she sat back on the bed, clad in her T-shirt and plain briefs. Boredom and fear. How in God's name did one fight boredom and fear in a square grey box? Her eyes drifted bleakly round the cell, then widened as they came to rest on the little black rectangle lying on the bed, beside where Wolf had been sitting.

The radio.

The next morning, a sullen-faced Senta brought Susie a simple breakfast of cereal and coffee. She stood in silence, watching her captive eat, her china-doll face incongruously contrasting with the squat machine-gun held across her body. She was wearing pseudo-military khaki breeches and a fawn blouse this morning, a heavy leather belt fastened round her waist. The guerilla-type clothing emphasised the boyish, gymnastic grace of her taut little body.

On instinct, Susie had hidden the radio under her pillow as soon as she heard the bolts being unfastened. Something told her that Senta would greatly enjoy taking the privilege away from her. And in leaving her the radio, Wolf had thrown her a lifeline—almost literally. The tiny set had lightened the lonely hours immeasurably. Most of the stations she had been able to get had been Italian or French, confirming her suspicion that she was being held in north-east Italy. It had been her clock, her companion. Late at night she'd even been able to get the BBC World Service. There'd been no mention of her kidnapping on the midnight news service before she'd fallen asleep.

'Okay, *liebchen*.' Senta gestured with the gun. 'You've filled your belly. Now move.'

'Where to?' Susie asked, as the other woman shepherded her out into the cellar beyond.

'To satisfy your bourgeois instincts for cleanliness,' Senta sneered. 'If it were up to me, you would rot in your own sweat and filth. But you are to be permitted to wash.'

The resentment in Senta's accented voice suggested strongly where the order had come from, but Susie made no comment.

The farmhouse was apparently empty but for the two of them. The old-fashioned rooms were sunlit, and the glimpse of fields and blue skies outside the many-paned windows was purgatory to Susie's yearning soul; but Senta jammed the muzzle of the sub-machine-gun into her back, forcing her up the stairs.

The bathroom, like the rest of the house, was old-fashioned but gracious. On the chair beside the vast bath was a small white towel and an old friend—the square airline bag Wolf had given her. Susie opened it eagerly. Bliss—her change of underwear!

'You have thirty minutes,' Senta said shortly. She hooked the chair over with one foot, and placed it squarely in the doorway, straddling it with the gun resting on the hooped back. 'I shall be watching.'

See if *I* care, Susie retorted inwardly. Ignoring Senta completely, she twisted the hot-tap all the way. A marvellous cascade of near-boiling water began to fill the tub. She went to the basin, and stared into the mirror. Her own appearance shocked her—she'd almost forgotten the bleach-and-haircut, and the bell of off-blonde hair was startling. Her oval face, though, showed little sign of the strain she'd been through, apart from smudges under her deep blue eyes. The summer tan made her look a lot healthier than she felt, contrasting with the crushed-strawberry of her generous mouth. What were they going to do when the real black started growing back into her hair?

Trying to forget that Senta's pale eyes were on her, she filled the basin, hauled off her shirt and jeans, popped them in, and scrubbed vigorously at them both with the bar of pink soap. Maybe Senta would let her dry them outside; they'd be able to dry out in her cell if necessary. She'd never been able to bear the feel of dirty clothes.

'What a little bourgeoise you are,' Senta sneered from the doorway. Susie glanced at her, feeling naked in her brief underclothes, especially with the threat of the gun between them. The other woman's face was twisted with dislike.

'What makes you hate me?' she asked casually, rinsing out the clothes.

'I hate what you stand for,' Senta retorted. 'Wealth, privilege, arrogance. You are corrupt.'

'Am I? I work for a living, like everybody else.' Susie draped the wet clothes over the basin, and went to test the bathwater. Senta didn't reply, her pale eyes studying Susie's tanned legs and slim waist in a deadly silence. Shrugging mentally, Susie pulled off her bra and briefs, and slipped quickly into the deliciously hot water.

It was uncomfortable to lie with the taps behind her—but that way she didn't have to look at Senta.

Ecstasy to be able to sink back, closing her eyes! Not even the knowledge that Senta was watching her could take away the delight of her first bath in days. There was even a small bottle of cheap shampoo, and she lathered her blonde mop, scrubbing her scalp as though to wash off the whole experience of the past three days. Then she washed the filmy undergarments, and rolled on to her stomach, feeling less exposed that way. The barred window looked up into a cloudless sky, and she stared dreamily at the blue square, lapped in the warmth of the water. What was Dad doing now? Telling the police for the thousandth time what had happened that morning? Sitting rigid at his desk, his lined eyes staring into space?

'Has my father been contacted yet?' she asked quietly. 'He'll be sick with worry.'

'You have no right to ask questions,' Senta snapped. 'And your sentimentality does not fool me, *liebchen*. Get out now.' As Susie rose, dripping, she went on savagely, 'In upper-class families like yours, ties of love do not even exist. That is well-known.'

Susie stared at the fanatical face for a second, almost pitying this twisted doll. She pressed the thin towel to her wet mouth.

'Sure,' she said gently. 'They don't even exist.'

'Your father has a kept whore,' Senta spat out.

Susie turned to face her, her movements slow. So much hate in one young mind. 'You know,' she said, 'you remind me of someone, Senta.'

'Who?' the blonde girl demanded.

'A schoolfriend of mine,' Susie replied, thinking of Greta Lang's spiteful little face. She, too, had been blonde and petite, though her eyes had been black, black as wet pebbles. 'Her name was Greta Lang, and she was always saying spiteful things about the other girls' parents. She took a delight in telling people how awful their mothers were, or that their fathers were having affairs with other women.'

'So?' Senta's narrowed eyes showed uneasy interest.

'No one really minded,' Susie said gently. 'Because everyone knew that Greta's parents had never wanted her. They'd been divorced for years, and she was living with relations. She was just taking her unhappiness out on others.' Senta's face paled swiftly, and for a moment, Susie thought she might strike at her—but the pale eyes stayed emotionless. 'Very interesting,' she said softly.

She dried herself as best she could while the water gurgled away, then indicated her wet jeans and shirt. 'What am I to do with these?'

'You chose to wash them,' Senta said vindictively, 'now you can wear them.'

'Can't they go in the sun for an hour?' Susie pleaded. 'It's a hot day, they'd be dry in no time.' She'd made the request without much hope, but to her astonishment, Senta paused, then nodded sharply.

'*Richtig*. Hang them on the line outside. And you can go in the sun too. For half an hour. You will wear your wet underclothes.'

Susie gaped for a second. The gleam in Senta's eyes puzzled her, but the offer was a lot too good to turn aside. Maybe what she'd said about Greta Lang had moved the girl in some way? She pulled on her bra and briefs again. The wet had made them transparent, but they would soon dry in the baking sun. And it meant she had a change with the ones in the bag. God, it was going to be good to feel the sun on her skin again!

Senta herded her down the stairs, and into the yard outside. It was blazingly hot, and the magnificent, lonely countryside all around lifted Susie's spirits like champagne. Senta jerked her gun at the clothes-line.

'Hang them there. You sit here. I will be watching from the porch.'

Wondering what miracle had prompted Senta's sudden access of humanity, Susie hung up her clothes and settled obediently on to the lush grass where Senta had indicated. The terrorist had settled herself in the shade of the porch, the ever-present gun lying across her knees. She was talking quietly in Italian into the slim walkie-talkie —some routine check or other. That pale skin, Susie guessed, would burn furiously in direct sunlight.

With a sigh of bliss, she lay back, feeling the sun's healing warmth soaking into her bare skin.

But for the fine underclothes, she was completely naked. Her nipples were visible through the wet silk, dark aureoles against the cream of her full breasts, but she'd never been self-conscious about her body. The fact that every man she'd met had told her it was beautiful had never made her vain; she'd been brought up to keep herself physically healthy, and she'd always enjoyed exercise—but Susan Cheyne was not in the habit of thinking about herself in directly sexual terms. If that was extraordinary in a twenty-two-year-old woman of singular loveliness, then perhaps the fact that her heart had never yet been stirred to any passion might provide an answer.

The sun was warm on her moist lids, and for the first time in days she felt the muscles of her face relaxing. The sunlight would bleach her hair even more, turning it to platinum. Maybe that was what had been in Senta's mind. Was anyone going to recognise her after all this? She thought of Joe, his gentle, smiling brown eyes. The way he'd kissed her the night before she'd left for Switzerland. Was she ever going to be the same again after this ordeal? Could she just walk back into the growing relationship she'd had with him?

Dear Joe. Thoughts of him brought back memories of Fairbourne, and the long, sweet crescent of white sand under the crumbling cliffs. . . .

A shadow fell across her face, and she opened her eyes lazily. Then sat up in sudden fear. Draco's looming shape was blotting out the sun, his brutal face leering down at her. There was an almost mad glint in the piggy eyes as they stared hungrily at her near-naked body.

Her heart thumping, Susie twisted round, and

got to her feet. She felt horribly exposed, her only thought to get back to the house.

'*Aspetta.*' His hand clamped on her wrist, jerking her round to face him. With his other hand, he let his shotgun fall on to the grass. He leered at her, his eyes hungry on the dark triangle of her sex, visible through the briefs.

'Let me go,' she demanded, trying to keep her voice steady. The broad-nosed face was animal-like in its lust. Susie looked desperately back to the porch.

Senta was gone.

God! So *this* was why her eyes had gleamed as she had offered the unexpected privilege. She had called Draco on the radio—and she would be watching now, Susie knew instinctively, from one of those dark windows, her pale eyes gleaming greedily. Senta was going to make her pay dearly for that story about Greta Lang! She twisted her arm frantically, but Draco pulled her closer with inexorable strength.

His hand groped at her breast as his mouth rooted for her lips, his bristly jowls scraping her skin painfully. His feral smell was overpowering, his breath sickening against her mouth. Terrified, Susie lashed her free fist into his ribs. Under the blubber, Draco's thick body was hard with muscle. He laughed softly at her futile pummelling, his imbecile grin showing rotten teeth. She screamed sharply as his fingers tightened viciously round her wrist, and tore herself desperately away from him.

'Leave me alone,' Susie panted. He took a step towards her, grinning wider, and she raked instinctively at his face. Her nails caught his arm, scratching red weals into the skin. His curse showed that she had hurt him this time.

'Io sono il padrone qui,' he growled. Anger flickered with the lust in his eyes as they devoured her near-naked body. Then, with surprising speed for such a big man, he grasped both her hands in his powerful paws, and jerked her on to the ground. She tried to twist away, mad with fear, but he dropped heavily on to her, imprisoning both her wrists in one hand. In a murderous silence, she struggled against him, her face white with terror. Rape had always been her worst nightmare, something which she feared more than death itself—and the bestial light in the piggy eyes above her left her in no doubt as to Draco's intentions. She strained her neck back, trying to bite his restraining hand. He growled softly, his breathing becoming faster with the exertion and the excitement of overcoming her. He leaned hard on her wrists, crushing them against the ground with one hand. With the other, he tore at her brassiere, exclaiming roughly as he exposed her breasts.

She had no breath to scream. Blackness began to flood her mind, her trembling muscles going limp with a kind of paralysing horror. There was a roaring in her ears, as though she were drowning. Through it, Susie heard Draco's triumphant laugh as he saw her eyes roll back in near-unconsciousness. With purposeful brutality, he forced her desperately clenched thighs apart.

CHAPTER FIVE

ABRUPTLY, the crushing body on top of her was hauled away.

Dazedly, Susie sat up, covering her breasts, feeling consciousness return to her aching mind. Wolf was standing between her and Draco, who was clumsily fastening his breeches. She gasped his name in relief.

'He—he was going to rape me,' she whispered huskily.

Wolf nodded curtly. His eyes were arctic green on the burly peasant, his lean body tense with anger.

'Go into the house,' he told her quietly, his eyes never leaving Draco's. Then, in the same soft voice, he asked Draco something in Italian. Draco turned his head aside and spat on to the ground without replying. His heavy features were dark with anger and frustrated passion.

Unsteadily, Susie stood up, fumbling with her twisted bra. Draco's hot eyes darted at her in hatred—and then, with that same deceptive speed, he stooped, and snatched the shotgun up from the grass beside him. Holding it by the barrel, he swung the heavy stock hard at Wolf's head, grunting with the force of the blow. Susie had no time to scream a warning.

Wolf didn't need one. He was sidestepping the killing blow almost before it was delivered, his eyes lethal green slits; and as the big man was trying to recover the gun for a second attack, he surged forward with a leopard's speed and grace, powerful hips lifting for the high kick that snapped into Draco's jaw with enough force to send him sprawling on to the grass, the shotgun tumbling out of his hands.

There was fear in the brutish face as Draco scrambled dazedly to his feet again, fists like hams raised to defend himself. Susie shrank back against the washing-pole in disbelief as she watched Wolf; his powerful body radiated violence as he stalked the bigger man. She hated violence, had never been able to watch men fighting without feeling sick to her stomach. God knew she didn't want Draco punished any more. There had been a terrifying expertise about that kick, a killer's honed skill. And Draco's flickering eyes might have been looking into his own grave as he backed away from the inexorable advance.

Suddenly baring his teeth, the peasant lunged forward, swinging both fists in a flurry of blows. None of them struck their target; but Wolf's fist lashed out, snapping the heavy head back on the thick neck for a second time. There was blood on Draco's face as he reeled away, curses spilling from his lips.

'Stop it!' Unable to bear the thought that he would kill Draco, Susie ran forward to Wolf, her voice pleading. 'Dear God, *don't*! He didn't hurt me——'

Draco rushed at Wolf, massive hands reaching for the other man's windpipe, bloodstained teeth bared like some wild animal's. With dreadful deliberation, Wolf sidestepped again; but this time he whipped his right fist like a piston into Draco's face. The terrible blow seemed to surge from his hips; it connected with a sound that made nausea flood Susie's throat. Draco's big body jolted as though he'd stepped on to a high-tension electric cable, and then he crumpled to the ground, limp as death.

Susie forced her silent scream back with both fists, sinking to her knees beside Draco.

'You've killed him,' she said in stunned horror. Casually, Wolf rolled the peasant over with his foot. Blood bubbled at the nose and gaping mouth.

'He'll live,' he commented dispassionately. He wasn't even breathing heavily, his lazy tiger's eyes iceberg-cold as he studied Draco briefly.

'We've got to get him into the house,' Susie said urgently, trying to control her heaving stomach. She knew very little about first-aid, but Draco was almost certainly going to be concussed when he came to.

'No,' Wolf commanded grimly. 'Let him fry out here in the sun. Get your clothes.' He scooped up the shotgun, and flung it easily into the waist-high grass of the adjoining meadow. With a glance at Susie's white face, he turned to the house. 'Come.'

She followed numbly, still unable to believe the explosive power that had erupted from Wolf's body. She held the wet clothes against her body, beginning to shiver in reaction to the horror of what had just happened. Senta was standing on the porch, her doll's face paler than ever. She seemed almost infantile as she clutched the sub-machine-gun, her eyes fixed on Wolf's.

'I take it this was your idea?' he asked softly as he came up the stairs to her.

'I—I wasn't watching,' Senta stammered, her eyes like a lying child's. 'I went for a drink, and the next thing——'

Wolf jerked the weapon out of her arms, uncocked it contemptuously, and tossed it through the doorway.

'She must have provoked him,' Senta said, fear widening her pale eyes as she stepped back. She pointed a shaking finger at Susie. 'Look at her, the bitch! She must have led him on——'

Susie squeezed her eyes shut in reflex as Wolf drew his hand back to lash across Senta's face; those hands had half-killed a man as big as Draco. Senta crouched away from her leader, bloodless lips writhing. Terror was naked in her face.

'Please,' Susie said shakily. 'No more.' This whole ghastly mess had started with her—what she'd said to Senta in the bathroom had cut deep enough to really hurt the girl. That was why she'd lured Draco to assault her. 'It was partly my fault, anyway.'

Wolf didn't unleash the blow. The threat had been enough.

'You're a fool, Senta,' he said in a voice like a whip. He lowered his arm slowly. 'You let personal feelings interfere with your work. That is a very bad habit. I advise you to lose it before it kills you.'

'*What about you?*' the blonde woman hissed. Her eyes were vindictive. 'Why do you protect this slut? You heard her admit it was her fault—she provoked me! She is your enemy——'

'We do not rape and torture,' he said, cutting through her quivering sentence. 'Leave that to the pigs in the employ of the State. This is the second time I've had to discipline you for unnecessary actions. The third time I will not be so lenient.'

'Yes.' Slowly, Senta stood upright, the tip of her tongue exploring her lips. 'We heard how tough you were, Comrade Wolf. A hard man.' Malice flickered in her humourless smile. 'Harder on your friends, it seems, than on your enemies.'

'You talk like a child,' he said indifferently.

'By rights, *I* should have been in charge of this operation,' Senta snarled. 'But *you* had to step in at the last moment, out of nowhere, and take everything over. I think I know why, now.' She stared contemptuously at Susie's half-naked body, then looked back into Wolf's silent face. 'So your tastes run to little bourgeoises, eh Comrade? Are the lure of wealth and a pair of brown legs really enough to distort the will of Red Dawn's most dangerous operative?'

'You've said enough,' Wolf rapped.

'I shall repeat what I have said to the Executive Committee,' Senta said viciously. 'I shall tell them what I think—that the man who killed Johann Weiss now spends his energies protecting a middle-class slut who has bewitched him.'

Wolf laughed contemptuously. 'You're fanciful, Senta.'

'Then why do you pamper her like this?' Senta asked urgently. Fear and anger had given way to pleading in the china-blue eyes. '*Lieber* Wolf, she stands for everything we are sworn to destroy— wealth, power, arrogance! What makes you want to shield her—if not that she has charmed her way into your pants?'

'Ah.' A slow smile curved across his sensuous mouth. 'I think I begin to understand why you are so irrational.' He reached out bronzed fingers to cup Senta's chin. 'You're jealous, my little Senta. Not so?'

'Why did you insist on commanding this

operation?' the blonde pouted, pushing his hand away. 'You think she is beautiful——'

Her eyes closed to adoring crescents as he drew her close, his mouth silencing hers with a fierce kiss. The taut, tennis-star body pressed hungrily against Wolf's balanced power.

Susie turned away, her face set.

Animals. Worse than animals—to embrace and kiss in the aftermath of horrifying violence. If she had feared Wolf before, she now hated him with a sick passion. These people were scarcely human. Senta's little noises of desire behind her made her clamp her hands to her ears, gritting her teeth. Animals.

Something Senta had said echoed through her mind. *The man who killed Johann Weiss.* The name was familiar from headlines and television newscasts. Johann Weiss, a grey-haired man in early middle age. Details drifted back. Head of some kind of anti-terrorist squad.

Blown to shreds in a savagely big car-bomb explosion. She lowered her hands slowly. She was remembering her father's anger at the outrage—it had happened only a few weeks ago, and the whole of Switzerland had been shocked. Wolf's claim to fame, the destruction of a defenceless man who had devoted his life to protecting his society from mad dogs like these.

Susie turned. Senta was disengaging herself from Wolf's bronzed arms. There was triumph in her flushed face as she glanced into Susie's ultramarine eyes.

'Wait,' she said huskily to Wolf, who was leaning against the door, green eyes smiling lazily. 'I'll take *her* below first.'

She hustled Susie down into the cellar, and

pushed her back into the grey cell.

'You see?' she asked, her doll's face bright. 'He feels nothing for you. And now I am going upstairs—so that he can make love to me.'

Susie didn't bother to retort. The door slammed, leaving Susie with the echoeless silence of her prison. She curled up on the mattress, pressing her knuckles into her eyes to shut out the memories of the things she'd seen this morning. She felt empty inside, as though there were not even pain left in her heart. A narcotic numbness that would, she knew, wear off all too soon. Wolf was a killer.

So what? She'd suspected that all along. *Killer*. The word was as ugly as the deed. Damn him, she thought suddenly, anger mingling with her pain, why did he have to kill? What in God's name had made him turn so much strength and capability to such a horrible end? Nothing had hurt her quite like that revelation. That betrayal.

She reached slowly, and pulled the little radio from under her pillow.

She pressed it to her cheek, waiting for the tears.

They didn't let her out of her cell again, except for brief visits to the toilet, for four days. In that time, she scarcely saw Wolf. Senta, slightly better-tempered since the Draco incident, or the other 'peasant', a taciturn red-headed man in his thirties, brought meals to her cell

Susie's life shrank to the confines of her grey prison.

Her initial fears and rages gave way, over the hours of solitude and loneliness, to a blank apathy. She lay back against the tiled wall, letting her mind wander along faraway beaches, or even further back, to childhood memories of holidays she and her mother and father had spent in the mountains, by the lakes, in forests. The batteries in the transistor radio grew weaker, and her only distraction faded away.

She hardly noticed.

She tried to keep her mind as far away from the present as she could. Thinking about her father and what he was going through only brought madness. So she kept her thoughts as far back in the past as she could. Schooldays in Edinburgh. Odd incidents from her childhood. Her mother seriously taking her aside to explain 'the facts of life' when she was nine. Her bored response—*'oh that* stuff! Everybody knows about *that* stuff'— becoming a family joke.

Nearly drowning in the sea off Brighton one summer, the choky feel of salt water in her lungs, the endless supplies of it in her tummy when an alert uncle fished her out and draped her over his knee to empty like a hot-water-bottle.

And once, when she was half-asleep, the memory of Wolf's warm mouth, the subtle fire of that slow smile, the unexpectedly clear, cool green eyes against his burned-honey skin. And she'd felt tears rising up. Tears that someone so strong and beautiful could be so evil. Tears at how badly she could miss someone as lethal as Comrade Wolf.

'You look like a ghost.' She blinked into wakefulness, and became aware of the tall figure standing at the doorway. Her heart lurched into a higher gear, thumping almost audibly against her chest. He came over to her, leaving the door open, and studied her dispassionately. Her first, almost uncontrollable, impulse was to grasp his hands and beg for some news of her father, plead for the slightest inkling of how he was, whether he even knew she was still alive or not. Instinct made her choke the questions back. She needed to know about her father too badly to waste any opportunity; maybe she could get what she wanted in a more subtle way.

'You're very pale,' he commented.

'It's all the sun I get,' she retorted wrily. He seemed to fill the room, his colours rich as sunlight against the monotonous grey. She wanted to reach out and touch the warm gold of his skin, touch some of the summer that seemed to cling to his body.

'I see you haven't lost your somewhat acerbic sense of humour.' He tilted her chin so that he could study her oval face by the weak light that never went off. His eyes were like rock pools, a sparkling green that invited her to lose herself in their depths, drown herself in him. . . .

She shook the thoughts away angrily. Confinement was making her lose her grip. She twisted her face away from his probing eyes, and hugged her knees.

'I haven't seen you for days.' The statement hovered somewhere between complaint and accusation.

'I've been busy,' he said flatly. She glanced at him from under thick lashes, her fear and dislike of him almost overcome by her deep pleasure in seeing him again. It wasn't just that, unlike Senta and the other man, he treated her like a human being; he was vivid, vital, utterly different from their colourless cruelty.

'How's Comrade Draco?' she asked coolly.

'Draco's no longer a Comrade,' he smiled. 'He's been relegated to the lower orders.' A tiny smile touched his lips. 'You were very stupid. I did warn you not to ask for anything or do anything unless I was there. Not so? Draco's all right,' he went on dismissively. 'He's been very polite lately.'

'No doubt,' she said drily. 'What was that stuff? Karate?'

'Something like that.'

She nodded, and glanced at him again. 'And how's Comrade Senta?'

'Flourishing.' The leopard's eyes challenged her mockingly, daring her to make any comment. 'She's been amusing herself by pulling the wings off butterflies.'

Despite herself, Susie smiled again. Their eyes met, and she shook her head in slow puzzlement. Had he felt triumph when he'd killed that man? Or just the satisfaction of a job well done?

'I don't understand,' she said quietly. 'You're so different from them, Wolf. So much—I don't know. Wiser. More mature. *Why?*'

'Why what?' he asked calmly.

'Why are you with them, doing all these terrible things? You're a million miles from Senta and Udo and Draco, and the others.'

'But my aims are very close to theirs.' He shrugged. 'Sometimes one has to work with poor materials, even rotten materials. The end justifies the means.'

'You really believe in all that rubbish they spout?' Susie challenged in disbelief. 'About the downtrodden millions, and society needing to be reshaped?'

'In essence,' he nodded, 'yes.'

'And you really believe crime and violence are the way to change society?'

'It's a war, Susan.' Intelligent eyes assessed her

coolly. 'It's only crime from the enemy's point of view.'

She took a deep breath. 'What you did to that man—Johann Weiss—you call that social change?'

His expression didn't alter by a millimetre.

'Who told you about Johann Weiss? Ah yes. Our dear Senta. Johann Weiss lived by the sword. He died by the sword.'

'He died horribly,' she snapped emotionally. 'And *you* planted the bomb. My father said that murdering him like that was worse than anything that had been done in the war.'

'Your father's factories made the explosive in that bomb.' The sharp retort made her wince painfully. 'No one is innocent,' he said more gently. 'We intend to struggle until the fight is won. There are few of us, but we are highly skilled, and totally dedicated. We are going to fight to the end. Now—let's talk about something else.'

She sat in silence, despairing at the vast gap that lay between them, a gap too wide for any emotion or thought to cross. 'What's your real name?' she asked impulsively.

He laughed softly. 'Wolf is my real name. Melodramatic, I agree, but nonetheless my own.' He rose fluidly. 'Some of the colour has returned to your cheeks. But you still look ill to me.' He considered, fist on hip. 'Perhaps I'd better arrange for you to have some time outside.'

'I embrace your feet, O Master,' she reacted sourly. But her heart had jumped with delight at the prospect of seeing the sun and breathing fresh air again. He dropped a square cellophane packet into her lap. Four batteries for the radio. She held them tight in her hand, and looked up at him.

'Are your—negotiations—going well?'

'Satisfactorily,' he nodded. God damn him—he was laughing at her anguish, somewhere deep in those cat's eyes.

'Wolf——' she pleaded desperately, 'my father—I've *got* to know how he is, whether you've contacted him yet——' She fought back the mistiness in her eyes. 'Does he know that I'm not dead? Please!'

'Your father has every reason to believe that you are alive,' he said coolly. Her entreaty seemed to have drawn a veil down over the warmth that had just been glinting in his eyes. 'You will shortly be able to tell him yourself that you are quite well.'

The colour drained from Susie's face, her heart beating so fast that she felt faint.

'You—you mean you're going to let me go?' she whispered.

'I'm afraid not,' he replied silkily. 'But it's part of our plan for you to communicate with him.'

'When?'

'Soon.'

Her hand had unconsciously reached for his, and now he pulled her slowly towards him. 'No more questions.' She stared up into his face, frozen by the sudden knowledge that he was going to kiss her. Her eyelids fluttered closed as he took her face in his hands. His mouth was unbelievably kind, sealing warmth around her instantly. For an instant she was still, stunned by the contact of their lips; and then she melted against him. It didn't matter any more, the pretence of keeping up her courage didn't matter. Their kiss opened into flaring need, and she dug her fingers into the hard muscles of his shoulders as his tongue found hers, sliding into her mouth in a shockingly sexual caress.

It was as though the bottom had dropped out of her world. The arousal in her body was an instant flood, a force that surged her against him helplessly, reaching for the comfort he had to offer. Her breasts were crushed against him, and she moaned like a cat as his hands bit into her flanks, sliding down the lean angles of her hips.

She was shaking like a leaf as he pulled back, eyes as bright as burning copper.

'I doubt whether that will make you feel any better,' he said softly. The mockery cut across her vulnerability like a lash, and she sat down on the bed, hating herself with sudden venom. He smiled down at her, indifferent, utterly male. 'I think that's called fraternising with the enemy, Susan.'

'Leave me alone,' she grated in a dry voice.

His laugh was soft, mocking, sexy. 'I thought you had better control of yourself. But I'm going.' At the door, he turned back. 'You kiss like a virgin. A very eager virgin.'

Her retort was unprintable.

She covered her face in her hands as he closed the door and bolted it. Disbelief and self-disgust were making her feel sick. God, she'd behaved like an animal on heat! Was she crazy? Yet the memory of how his body had felt, hard and male, surged through her mind again, and she whispered a curse as her stomach tightened helplessly with desire.

The horrible truth was undeniable. She hated him, yet she wanted him so badly. So very badly that her body was quivering like a violin-string.

And it hurt even more to have to admit that she had never felt a fraction of that in Joe Dowson's arms. Not even a pale shadow of that.

Exhaling, Susie lay back on the bed, trying to

relax. None of the expletives she could find summed up her feelings. She had been betrayed, and by her own body. The tender, wet ache in her loins was a torment. She curled up into a ball, and tried to force her mind away from the memory of his mouth and the gaze of those leopard eyes.

From what he'd said, her father might already have been contacted. Maybe they'd sent him that picture Senta had taken in front of the flag. She imagined her father studying the pale, tired face, and grimaced.

What had he meant by 'communicate'? Surely not a telephone call? Her pulses leaped at the thought of hearing her father's voice again, being able to tell him not to worry, that she was in good health. The thought was too precious to dwell on. She rolled on to her stomach, slotted the new batteries into the radio, and curled up again with the comforting trickle of music at her ear.

There wasn't any sense hating herself for what had happened just now. There was something incredibly exciting about his presence, a blend of danger and attraction that was like a fire in her blood. There probably wasn't a woman in the world who could be indifferent to Comrade Wolf. He probably hadn't wanted to humiliate her. She'd humiliated herself. And now he would know just exactly how readily her body would respond to him. Mingled fear and anticipation sparked in her. Would he take advantage of that?

Probably. Comrade Wolf wasn't exactly a gentleman. She hadn't even thanked him for the batteries, she realised inconsequentially.

So what? The man was a killer, she reminded herself sharply. He had forced her from her father's house at gunpoint, imprisoned her, exposed her to mind-bending fear and tension. Any little acts of humanity he might commit had to be weighed in the scale against the darker, more terrible things he had done. Murder, kidnapping, extortion.

That was the sort of man Comrade Wolf was.

But she couldn't resolve the question as easily as that. Thoughts of him nagged at her, refusing to leave her alone. She lay lost in thought for an hour, her cheek pillowed against her arm, trying to work out what might drive a man like Wolf to turn against society, become a predator upon it. Her ideas about urban terrorists had been fairly simple up till now. They were either dedicated Trotskyites whose lives had been so badly distorted by poverty and bad luck that they could no longer believe in peaceful political change—or there were the other kind, the spoiled children of rich middle-class people who had turned to violence out of some terrible boredom.

Wolf, clearly, was none of these. He had an authority that was utterly lacking in the others—a dangerous maturity that marked him out as a very special man. He was deadlier than any of the others—quite different, as a leopard is different from house-cats—and yet he had been infinitely kinder than any of them. There had been the little touches, like the radio, that had probably saved her sanity. And Wolf's authority was of the kind that usually belonged to the other side of the political coin. The authority of someone who had wealth or power, or both, someone who did a demanding job supremely well. Had Wolf defected from some high echelon of business, maybe from law, or even medicine?

It was useless to speculate. She tried to muster

her hatred of him again. But in this tiny world she was locked into, there weren't any standards any more. She could only measure Wolf against Senta, or Draco. Compared to them, he was at least not warped or brutish. Compared to someone like her father. . . .

She slammed the thought away, suddenly terrified by the thought that she was becoming as fascinated by Wolf as a bird with a cobra.

CHAPTER SIX

SOME hours later Susie heard the bolts being unfastened again, and hastily thrust her radio under the pillows. It was Senta—looking, to Susie's relief, more businesslike than malicious. She thrust a sheet of paper into Susie's hands, and sat on the bed beside her, setting the controls on a small portable cassette-recorder.

'You will read what is written on that paper. Aloud,' she commanded. Before Susie even had time to see what the message was about, Senta had switched the machine on to 'Record', and was holding a small, cheap microphone to her lips.

'I'm not going to read this,' Susie snapped, tossing the paper down. The vicious glitter of metal made her jerk back. The flick-knife in Senta's hands was razor-sharp, and behind it her pale eyes were livid with anger.

'You think Wolf will protect you from everything,' she hissed. 'You are wrong.' Susie gasped as the blade darted forward, the needle-tip stinging her throat like a bee. She touched the place, and stared at the blood on her fingers in disbelief. Evidently the Greta Lang story had been neither forgotten nor forgiven.

'Next time I will really hurt you.' Senta closed the knife, wound the spool back, and set the machine again. Her whole body rigid with anger, Susie picked up the paper, and read what was on it in a flat monotone.

'"The corrupt, exploitative capitalist system is

coming to an end,''' the statement began. She winced at the banal revolutionary phrases, and went on, '''Workers of the world, unite! You have nothing to lose but your chains. We in Alba Rossa are striking yet another blow for your freedom. Join us. Together we will create the New Utopia, the promised world of universal freedom, peace and happiness.''' Her eyes met Senta's ironically, but the terrorist simply jerked the microphone, indicating that she shouldn't stop. '''I am well,''' she started again. '''I have been treated kindly and with consideration. To the press of the world I have this to say: Alba Rossa represents the new dawn of humanity. Stop telling lies about them—they are the spearhead of the great proletarian revolution. To my father——''' her voice suddenly faltered as she came to the words '''—to my father I have this to say: co-operate with Alba Rossa, and all will be well. Long live Marx. Long live Lenin. Long live the Revolution.''' The message came to an end, but before Senta could switch the machine off, Susie said, her voice low and tense with urgency, 'I love you, Daddy.'

Senta's face was angry as she switched the cassette-player off.

'Stupid bitch,' she spat out, snatching the paper away from Susie. But, apparently satisfied with what she'd recorded, she stalked out without another word.

Susie found herself shaking in the aftermath of the recording. It had been a strangely emotional experience. Almost like really talking to her father, even though the medium had been Senta's tape-recorder. She prayed that they wouldn't edit off her last sentence. That, more than anything, was what she wanted to tell him. Whether she lived or died, whether they met again in this world or not, she wanted him to know that she was thinking of him, and loving him.

The radio told her it was night, and she slept. Again, she dreamed of Canada, and the surging Atlantic. Except instead of being grey, it was now green. Vivid, sparkling green.

She was still lying in bed the next morning, naked but for her briefs, half-asleep, when the door next opened. It was Wolf, dressed in the rough leather waistcoat, boots and cap of a peasant. There was a shotgun slung over his shoulder, and a belt of cartridges over the other. She sat up with beating heart, drawing the sheets to her chin, and stared at him in wide-eyed silence.

'Get dressed,' he commanded.

'Not in front of you,' she retorted. His grin was a sabre-flash of white in the tanned face.

'Come on—we're going out.'

'*Out?*' The mockery in his green eyes couldn't stop her flash of hope.

'You haven't got much time.' He obviously wasn't going to turn away to let her dress, and after a sceptical glare at him, she clambered out of bed, covering her breasts with her folded arms, and turned her back on him to dress.

'You really mean it?' she asked, wondering whether this was another cruel trick.

'Of course.'

'Where to?' she wanted to know, stepping into her jeans.

'Out. Your father got that tape yesterday.'

She spun round, deep blue eyes wide, and covered her breasts too late, knowing he'd caught a glimpse of her dark, taut nipples.

'Is that the truth?' she asked him quietly. He nodded, leaning negligently against the doorpost.

'It's the truth. The *whole* tape.'

She turned away, her face colouring. So he'd left her little private message on it! She pulled her bra and T-shirt on, and faced him, a little flushed.

'Can I wash and brush my hair before we leave?'

'No one's going to see you,' he said indifferently. 'Except me.'

'And you don't care.' The words held a hint of a question in them; she'd seen his gaze flicker to her breasts a minute ago, and she knew she must look strange, with her dishevelled clothes and bleached, cropped hair. He shook his head, an ironic smile lurking in his eyes.

'No, I don't care, Susie. Let's go.'

She padded on bare feet in front of him through the basement, and up the stairs. At least her father had heard her voice now, and knew she was alive. That thought was very warming indeed.

The house appeared to be deserted, and the remains of a meal were spread on the unpainted deal table. She glanced longingly up the stairs to where the bathroom was, and made an imploring expression in his direction.

'All right,' he nodded. 'You've got five minutes.'

She ran. It was bliss to use running water again; ablutions in a plastic bucket were dismal to say the least, and it was marvellous to rinse her skin clean. She even washed her bra and pants, figuring that they'd dry on her body. In the chipped and flaking mirror, her reflection was unfamiliar. There seemed to be a pallor under her tan now, and the delicate lines of her collar-bones and shoulders confirmed that she'd lost weight. She studied her own body, wondering whether Wolf would find her as attractive as Senta. Her breasts were smaller now, and sharper, and her hips were frankly bony. She hadn't noticed it, but the once-tight jeans now fitted comfortably.

Her face, she had to admit, had benefited by losing some weight. The model-like curves of her cheekbones would have looked stylish in a Rome studio, and her chin was as neat as a schoolgirl's. She smiled wrily at herself. She'd been wanting to lose weight, hadn't she? The rest of her wasn't very stylish, though. The black was already beginning to creep into the roots of her hair. She hoped Senta wasn't going to put her through another peroxide ordeal. She washed her face, thinking idly what a touch of rouge would do for her cheeks.

There was a laundry-basket in the otherwise bare bathroom and, on a sudden impulse, she peered inside it. All it contained were a few garments that obviously belonged to Senta—lacy panties, jeans, and a pair of nylon tights. She picked up the tights, a squiggle of nerves alive in her stomach. They might just possibly be useful— did she dare?

She stuffed them into her pocket with shaking fingers. It was a tiny act, but significant to her. Her first real opportunity to disobey the rigid laws of her captivity. Would Wolf be able to tell by the expression on her face? Would Senta notice that the tights were missing?

She put the lid back on the basket, raked her hair nervously into some kind of order, and went down the stairs to face Wolf. The small crime felt like a blazing mark on her forehead, and she decided that the best form of defence was probably attack.

'Why the fancy-dress?' she demanded, pointing

at his clothes. He looked like something out of a Victorian painting—The Gamekeeper, very macho and sultry.

'Camouflage,' he said neutrally. In fact, the peasant clothes suited him magnificently; the russets and browns of the rough cloth gave him a rangy look, and his mahogany skin confirmed the impression of a European countryman—a half-wild hunter or gamekeeper from some remote hillside.

'A Wolf in shepherd's clothing,' she said scathingly.

'That's right. Come.'

'But where are we going?' she persisted as he walked her to the door.

'I promised you an outing. Just enjoy it.' She stepped out into the sun. It was a beautiful morning, hot and still, and the instant spell of summer was magic after her imprisonment. Half-drugged with the sun, she tamely let him lead her to the battered Fiat pick-up which was parked in the yard.

They drove straight up the rough track that led towards the hills, Susie just drinking in her first glimpse of the outside world for days. It was almost like being back at work, free and untroubled. The countryside was completely deserted, barely a farm in sight; only a few smudges of smoke here and there suggested that there were people living in the region. The scenery confirmed her suspicion that she was being held in Italy; beautiful and rough, the countryside seemed to have the sweetness that she associated with Italy.

Within a few minutes, he swung the car off the track, and across the bumpy hillside. The broom

was in flower, a blaze of yellow against dark green,
and the grass was bright with wild flowers. So
happy that she felt she could easily have cried, she
stared at it all with hungry eyes. After the greyness
of her cell, this riot of colour and shape was
almost dizzying!

Over the brow of the hill, Wolf stopped the car,
and they got out. It was a lovely spot, an outcrop
of smooth rock making a perfect sun-trap among
the clumps of broom. It was also, she noticed
wrily, invisible from anywhere else.

'Where are we?' she asked, eyes half-closed
against the delicious sun.

'Don't be so full of questions,' he retorted. 'I
want you to get some sun, Susan. And some fresh
air.'

'Keeping the prisoner in peak condition?' she
asked cynically. But she was already stooping to
pick a wild flower at her feet. An almost childish
delight was in her. It was hot, the morning was
sweet with birdsong, and the grass was pleasantly
coarse under her bare feet.

It was wonderful to be able to forget the ordeal
she was going through. The place was thick with
flowers, and she soon had a bright posy in her fist.
She showed it to Wolf, who nodded indifferently.
He was leaning against the truck, watching her
with narrowed eyes.

Comrade Wolf wasn't interested in flowers, she
thought. She shrugged, and reached up to stretch
blissfully in the sun. There was something
saturnine about him, something dark and mocking
that seemed never to recede. She could feel his eyes
on her, felt with a woman's instinct that he was
assessing the lines of her body as she moved,
tasting the thought of her as a partner in bed.

Bastard. Yet it was an idyllic place; but for the shotgun still slung over his shoulder, she thought wrily, they might have been a pair of lovers on a picnic.

'Don't wander too far,' he growled.

'I wouldn't dare,' she retorted. But it was all too easy to imagine that she was free, and simply obey her impulse to run.

Susie sat on one of the sun-warmed rocks, absently arranging the flowers in her little bouquet. Freedom was so close, tantalisingly close! If she could somehow get into the car, perhaps by knocking Wolf senseless with a rock—she glanced across at him guiltily, half-believing he could read her thoughts. But he was opening a flask of coffee, paying her no attention.

Nerves twisted inside her at the line her thoughts were taking. Wolf was a killer. But if she took him utterly by surprise? The stockings! She could feel them, lumpy in her pocket. Such a flimsy advantage—but he didn't know she had it. She could fill one end with sand, and hit him with it. That was what they called a sandbag, wasn't it?

Derision at her own mad scheme made her get up restlessly. Wolf glanced up at her.

'Come and get some breakfast,' he commanded, squatting in the grass. He'd brought brioches and some fruit, and the mug of black coffee was steaming a welcome. Dragging her feet, she obeyed. This glimpse of freedom was too cruel. How could she face her cell again after this?

She knelt in the grass in front of where he was sitting cross-legged, and watched his hands as he tore one of the little cakes in two, offering her half. Strong hands, with long, capable fingers. She took the brioche he gave her. His tanned skin was velvet-fine, she noticed. He hadn't shaved, and the jet-black stubble gave him a savage, untamed look. Yet the long, dark lashes would have made any woman green with envy, and the wild green eyes were startlingly beautiful. He radiated male sexuality, and she dropped her eyes from his stare, crumbling the sweet bread in her fingers.

'What's Joe Dowson like?' he asked casually. Susie's head lifted up at the name.

'How d'you know about Joe?' she demanded, disturbed.

'I told you—we're very thorough.' His eyes were hooded as they assessed her expression. 'He's a PhD, isn't he? A good scientist?'

'One of the best,' she said shortly.

'You miss him?'

'Of course I do.' Damn! She didn't want to talk about Joe with this man—that was too personal a subject, and too fraught with pitfalls. 'Can we talk about something else?'

'Do you love him?'

'That's none of your business,' she snapped angrily. The last thing she needed was to give him yet another subject to tease her on. 'Joe's just a friend, that's all.'

'I don't believe any man could be just friends with you,' he said obliquely. 'Unless he was a eunuch.'

'Joe's no eunuch,' she retorted, knowing he was needling her deliberately.

'So.' He passed her a mug of coffee. 'He's your lover, then?'

'What the hell is it to you?' she wanted to know. 'Why all the questions?'

'I'm just interested.' The sunlight was carving a golden arabesque down the line of his face, and his eyes were as clear and deep as the green ocean she'd dreamed about last night. Out of nowhere came the thought that she'd like to photograph him, here, like this. He was physically so perfect, so intriguingly beautiful. It was an image she suddenly wanted to possess, always.... 'What are you staring at?' he asked over his coffee-mug.

'Nothing,' she said, looking away with an effort. It was time to clear her head. 'What kind of interest could you possibly have in me?' she asked, trying to inject acid back into her voice. 'I'm a corrupt little capitalist, no?'

'I like you,' he said calmly.

'You *like* me?' Her jaw dropped open. Of all the things to say! '*You* like *me*?'

'You're courageous and resourceful,' he observed, eyes on her mouth. 'You've got brains, too. Politics don't enter into that.'

'I'm glad to hear it.' She was still rather stunned. *Like?* She could have understood hate, or maybe lust, but *like*? It was almost disappointingly mild a term, and she didn't care if that *was* a vain thought. 'I think I'd rather have ferocious hatred! Anyway, I thought you just said no man could just be friends with me?'

'I think you're very desirable,' he said, smiling slightly. This time, she dropped the brioche, and simply stared, her face pink. 'Is that so extraordinary?' he asked innocently.

She didn't answer. That casual phrase had knocked the wind out of her sails completely. She picked up the cake in fumbling hands, and looked at it as though it were something from Mars.

'No butter?' she mumbled in protest.

'It's bad for the heart,' he commented, the smile in the tails of his eyes showing he was laughing at

her embarrassment. 'But there's some in the van if
you really want it.'

Susie nodded, and rose to get it. Desirable. The
word opened an entirely new phase of her
relationship with Wolf, and not one she could look
at with any equanimity, either. She had to walk
behind him to the van, and found herself staring at
the steering-wheel.

With heart-stopping suddenness, it occurred to
her that now was her chance! Everything else
evaporated from her mind. She was weak-kneed
with nerves as she peered at the ignition.

The keys weren't in it.

Wolf was a professional, she reminded herself
bitterly. The keys would be safe in his pocket.
With the butter in her hand, she turned around.
His broad back was to her, vulnerable and
unconcerned. The shotgun was propped against a
boulder next to him. If ever she was going to strike
at him, now was the moment. But she couldn't. If
it had been Senta sitting there, she'd have had no
compunction—but Wolf, Wolf who'd kissed
her——

The memory of the grey prison-cell rose up in
her mind. And the memories of all the cruel things
they'd done to her over the past weeks. The way
they were making her father suffer.

A red mist swept across her eyes. And then she
was acting on sheer instinct, her mind flooded with
anger. She put the butter quietly back on the seat,
pulled Senta's tights silently from her pocket, and
twisted the ends tightly round her fists, looping the
remaining two feet to make a crude garrotte. If she
could just disable him long enough to get the keys,
and run——

The blood was pounding in her ears as she

gritted her teeth, and took the three long steps to where Wolf was sitting. In one movement, she flicked the nylon loop over his head, round his throat, and pulled it tight with every ounce of strength in her body.

CHAPTER SEVEN

IT was as though she'd landed on a tiger's back.

His lean body surged with a savage power, rolling forward. Only the terror of what he would do to her if she let go made her cling desperately to the tights. He hauled her forward in a ferocious silence, his hands grappling with the noose around his throat. His elbow smashed into her ribs, flooding her mind with black pain, but she tore at the tights with all her power, desperately twisting to keep out of the way of further blows. The one thought in her mind was to bring him down, choke the air out of his lungs, before he fought free and destroyed her.

They slid to the ground in a tangle. He rolled her over, his back crushing her against the earth; she could feel the steel-taut muscles of his body straining against her, bucking against the noose that was strangling out his life. Sobbing, she clung to the nylon, feeling it cutting into her hands. If she could just hold on for the precious moments it would take——

Their bodies poised in a quivering arc for long seconds. She knew he was trying to force his fingers through the noose that was biting into his neck. Again, he surged up and back, slamming her against the rocks so that she felt as though her ribs were cracking. Blind and sick with fear and shock, Susie knew her hold on the impromptu garrotte was slipping. He would kill her if she failed, she knew that. They sprawled across the

106

rocks, their clothes and flesh scraping as they rolled. The cartridges in the belt around him dug painfully into her ribs. He staggered desperately to his feet, dragging her with him. She felt his hips slam backwards suddenly, knocking her off balance. And then, steel fingers clamped round her right arm. His hard shoulder dug into her armpit, and she had time for one sharp scream before he jerked her forward like a catapult. There was a split-second of disbelief in her mind as she knew she was cartwheeling through the air, over his shoulder. He kept his hold on her arm, twisting her as she fell.

Contact with the earth was devastating, a gigantic kick that swatted the air out of her lungs. Nauseous, she rolled over, her right side one fierce, aching bruise, and knew it was all over.

Wolf was gasping for air, the breath harsh in his bruised throat. He dropped to his knees beside her, pulling the tights from around his neck. She picked herself up weakly on one elbow. The dark blood was slowly draining from his face, and his chest was heaving to restore the oxygen to his lungs.

'Sweet God,' he whispered painfully, massaging his throat. 'You were trying to kill me!'

'No,' she panted, sweat crawling across her white face. 'I just wanted to get away—I had to do it——' She broke off on a gasp as the pain in her side swelled sickeningly. 'Oh, God,' she moaned. 'I had to do it. . . .'

His breathing steadier, Wolf pulled the cartridge-belt off, and leaned across her, his fingers biting into her pulse.

'Are you badly hurt?' he asked huskily, green eyes bloodshot.

Susie shook her head, tears blinding her eyes. He rolled her carefully over, his long fingers exploring her ribs with gentle, expert touches. She didn't care if he smashed her to pieces now. He would have every right to. She'd attacked him with the savagery of any animal. The thought that she'd come near to killing him was the most horrible thing of all. Remorse and horror choked her suddenly. She looked up, and touched his throat with her fingers, horrified to see the dark bruise already forming against the golden skin. Her mark. She'd hurt him—Wolf, the only man she'd ever felt any real passion for. Had she been insane? Her sobs came harshly, rackingly, and he gathered her in his arms, holding her close. What was happening to her? She'd never felt such conflicting passions, tearing her apart. . . .

'Oh, Wolf,' she wept, 'I didn't want to hurt you. I swear I didn't. I just had to do *something*.'

'Hush now.'

'What can I do to make it better?' she pleaded, like a child, misery making her more wretched than she'd been throughout the whole spell of her confinement.

'Nothing. It doesn't hurt.' He cradled her head against his chest while she cried her tears out. The birds, which had stopped singing during the life-and-death struggle of a few minutes ago, took up their songs again.

'You got the stockings from the washing-basket?' he asked. She nodded. 'I've under-estimated you before,' he said quietly. His voice was still ragged, and she looked up at him, her eyes huge and dark in her pale face.

'Are you all right?' she asked in a small voice.

'You didn't do my windpipe any good,' he

observed wrily. 'I'll live.' He got up to fetch the
flask, and they shared the last of the lukewarm
coffee from the same mug.

'Are you going to do something to me?' she
asked timidly, all the violence in her purged now.

He arched one dark brow. 'Like what?'

'I don't know. Hit me. Punish me for what I did.'

'Why?' A tired smile etched itself across his
mouth. 'I should have expected something like
that. We're enemies, after all. No matter how
desirable we find each other.'

'I didn't want to hurt you,' she said again,
desperate for him to believe her. He gave her a
sceptical look.

'You should have gone for the shotgun,' he
suggested drily. 'Then you could really have done
some damage.'

She winced, and stared dully down at herself.
She was filthy, her jeans torn and her T-shirt
stained with the frantic sweat of what had just
happened. It was still hard to believe that such a
murderous rage had come over her. Since that
day by the lake, the intense weeks had shown her
things in herself she'd never have dreamed possible
in a million years of ordinary life. Shown her sides
of Susie Cheyne that no one or nothing could ever
have revealed.

That she could even try and kill another human
being. A human being so very close to her.

'I'm sorry,' she said helplessly. 'I'm so very
sorry, Wolf.' He reached out, brushing the hair
out of her face. She looked up at him. The green
leopard's eyes were narrowed, his mouth com-
pressed in a tight, passionate line. 'Wolf,' she
whispered. She could feel the need in him, wild
and strong, calling to her inmost soul.

With a gasp, she was in his arms, his mouth claiming hers with ruthless mastery. It was unbearably sweet to feel him roll on to her, pressing her into the aromatic grass. He muttered her name, his voice growling deep in his chest, his kisses hot on her eyelids, her cheeks, her open mouth. The rough clothes he wore thwarted her fingers at first, until she found her way under them, her hands sliding across the warm, muscular flesh of his back. Their bodies were moving with urgency again, but not with violence now. As his tongue tasted the erotic secrets of her mouth, his thigh slid between hers, his hips thrusting forward in a primaeval movement to which her own body, needing no teaching, responded instinctively.

He paused only to haul his shirt off, his magnificent torso tawny in the sunlight. She was shuddering as he kissed the tender line of her jaw, his teeth almost brutal against her throat, biting at the slender muscles of her shoulders. Hunger was surging inside her, a need that only he could fulfil. His desire for her was barely controlled, her own body so slight and frail against his strength that he could have crushed her. Her fingers knotted in his thick hair as he kissed the valley between her breasts. She arched to let him unfasten her bra. He cupped her small breasts in his hands, kissing the dark peaks hungrily, his tongue and lips forming them into aching desire, one after another.

She pulled him to her, shameless in the depth of her passion for him, hugging his face against her breasts, feeling the stubble of his jaw rough against the satiny skin. She wanted to give herself to him, the passion in vivid contrast to her recent hatred.

As though she could heal the violence in her, heal the harm they'd done each other, by an act of love.

Wolf's movements became slower, mocking her own rising urgency. He kissed the smooth skin of her stomach, his tongue probing the oval dip of her navel on the way down to the flinching skin of her abdomen. She was moaning softly as he unfastened the copper button of her jeans, easing them over her hips so that only her flimsy briefs came between him and the centre of her need. Desire ran like flaming wine along her veins; there was no thought of enmity now, only the earth-born need between man and woman, the pure, clean desire that rose above all other passions.

He gathered her in his arms, kissing her hard enough to crush her answering lips, his hands roaming across her breasts, her flanks, the lean line of her hips.

'God, I need you,' he said huskily. His eyes, narrow and smoky smiled fiercely into hers. His fingers caressed her inner thighs in agonisingly slow circles, making her yelp softly as she squirmed down, her teeth nipping at the hard muscles of his arm. No man had ever done this to her before, but there was no fear in Susie's mind any more. She trusted him utterly, was utterly certain that she wanted him, wanted this man to take her here and now.

The touch of his fingers between her thighs was an unbelievable, heart-melting pleasure that made her bend like a bow against him, the breath swelling her lungs. With expert gentleness, he found the taut centre of her need, his caress driving all thought out of her mind in a flood of adoration. Pleasure peaked unbearably in her, her trembling muscles telling him how ready she was.

She didn't need to ask him; he was tugging off his denims, his own body big with need. As he knelt between her thighs, he smiled down at her, a mysterious, beautiful smile.

'Susie,' he said softly. 'Susie. . . .'

She reached out shakily to touch him. His neck arched back for a second; then, powerful as a bronze god of the glade, he was reaching for her, taking her to him.

On her lips his name was a prayer, an entreaty, a poem.

The radio-newscast came to an end. Wars and more wars. There had been no mention of the kidnapping. Susan Cheyne had slid off the front pages, and into oblivion. The cheerful pop-music that followed the news sounded ephemeral to her, unreal. No one cared. No one cared at all.

She switched off the radio, and lay curled up against the wall, her eyes dreamy with thought. Changes, changes. There had been more changes in these past weeks than in a whole lifetime. Someone had put his hand into her life, and pulled it inside-out.

How did other women feel, in the aftermath of love? Did they, too, feel this confusion, this inability to tell right from wrong? Wolf had taken her innocence, there in that glade this morning. Or had she given it to him? The question was immaterial. They'd made love, naked and fierce in the grass. She could feel the ache in her where he'd been, and her eyes closed involuntarily as she remembered the feel of his body inside her, the way he'd crushed her in his arms, gasping her name as his hardness thrust deep towards her womb, their minds and bodies becoming one wonderful experience. And the sunburst that had exploded between them, starting deep inside her, catching him up in the release, her own aching cry as she felt the scalding gift of his sex to her.

While it had lasted, it had been transcendent. A wonderful, infinitely good thing. Should she hate herself now, in the light of reason? She opened her heavy lids, aware of the sharp pains throughout her body. Pains of bruised ribs, cut skin, torn muscles. Pains of afterlove. There were no spiritual pains, though. Didn't she regret what had happened? It was easier to let her mind alone now, simply to be. She didn't want to examine her feelings, didn't want to know how much Wolf meant to her. She didn't want to start hating herself.

Somehow, a conscience seemed a crazy thing to have in a tiny grey prison.

But how would they judge her, the people on the outside, if they ever knew that she'd let her kidnapper make love to her this morning, in a glade of sunlight? She bit her bruised lip. No one would ever be able to understand. Least of all Joe. *Joe*. Her mind shied away from the thought of him. Joe had been one of things she'd clung to over the past weeks, an image of love and gentleness that had helped to sustain her. And hadn't she just betrayed him, in the most brutal possible way?

'No,' she whispered, almost on a gasp of pain. It hadn't been a betrayal. Making love with Wolf had been something she'd needed to do, needed more intensely than almost anything she could remember. It had nothing to do with Joe, and Joe must never know, not ever!

What had happened had been overwhelmingly

important to her. But she was going to have to
keep the secret hidden, for ever if needs be. It had
revealed, at the very least, how profoundly deep
her feelings for Wolf went, and she was mature
enough to recognise that her feelings for Wolf
were crazily exaggerated. A kind of hysteria built
up by loneliness and fear, something that had
needed to explode in the wild, pure act of sex with
him. He'd made her a woman, in the most
wonderful, thrilling way—but it was exclusively
physical. Physical, that was all. Wasn't it?

She couldn't help wondering what it had meant
to Wolf himself, though. They'd been silent on the
drive back to the farmhouse. She'd lain against
him, her head pillowed on his shoulder. The
feeling in her then had been a high that no alcohol
or drugs could have induced. A sense of deep joy,
of being way, way above the clouds. Slowly, she'd
come down, reality creeping into the summery
light of her feelings. But Wolf's face had been dark
and saturnine again, cynical lines harsh around his
mouth. When she caressed his hair, curling the
crisp, short darkness round her fingers, he hadn't
even blinked.

Only as he took her back to the cell did it dawn
on her that he wasn't experiencing the sentimental
euphoria she felt. There was no tenderness in him.
He'd been almost rough as he pushed her through
the door, and there hadn't been the slightest trace
of emotion in the vivid green eyes.

A deep sadness spread through her. To her it
had been the most important, most beautiful
experience of her womanhood—purely in a
physical sense, of course. To him? A casual thrill
with a captive. Maybe just a kind of recompense
for the hurt she'd done him. Certainly nothing

more. She couldn't help being hurt by that thought.

Would Joe ever make her feel what Wolf had given her this morning? The thought had entered her mind unbidden, and she thrust it angrily away. What was she, some kind of cheap harlot, comparing the possible performances of the men in her life?

She picked up the radio, trying to dismiss sudden turbulence in her mind. How long had she been here—sixteen days? Eighteen? She didn't know. Long enough to go half-crazy, anyway. This morning she'd tried to kill a man. And a few minutes later that man had made love to her, taking her soul beyond the reaches of ecstasy. Who would ever understand the logic of it? Wry lines creased around her eyes. Only someone who'd been kidnapped by a man like Comrade Wolf. She stood up, gathering her hair at the back of her neck. She was adult now. He'd given her that with his body, his desire. Oddly, she now felt more capable of facing her ordeal than ever before. Somehow, Wolf had given her something that chased the shadows out of her fears. She had discovered that she was capable of violence. And capable of love.

The sound of the bolts being unfastened made her turn slowly to face the door. The figure in the doorway was Senta's, her neat tennis-star's body rigid with anger. Her pale blue eyes raked Susie up and down, taking in the tear in her jeans, the marks of grass and earth on her clothes.

'What have you been doing?' she asked in a cold fury. Susie dropped her hands, watching the other woman warily.

'What could I have been doing?' she asked mildly.

'Wolf's neck is bruised,' Senta spat out savagely. Her mood was dangerous, and though she didn't seem to be armed, Susie felt her own tired muscles bracing for an onslaught. 'How did those marks come to be on your clothes?' she demanded.

'I rolled in the grass,' Susie replied.

'In the grass?' The ice-blue eyes narrowed in disbelief. 'He took you *outside*?'

Susie nodded. It hadn't occurred to her that Wolf's decision to take her out might have been made without the consent of the others, but Senta's quivering anger made her guess that now. The terrorist stepped forward, her fingers curling into claws.

'What happened between you?' she whispered.

'Ask Wolf,' Susie challenged. She was uneasy. Senta's feelings about Wolf were obviously intense; if she knew he'd made love to her, her reactions could be lethal.

'Did you hurt his neck like that?' Senta asked, her little white teeth showing like fangs.

'It was an accident.' The words came instinctively to her lips. Somehow she knew Wolf would have lied to the others about her attack—if only to protect her from retribution

'You're lying,' Senta snarled. 'You and Wolf both. What kind of accident?'

'Why don't you ask Wolf?' Susie repeated, her eyes still watchful on Senta's face.

'He made love to you!' The accusation burst out almost hysterically, and Susie felt her face tighten. That was one thing she *couldn't* lie about. She turned away stiffly, not answering. 'You've blinded him.' Senta's accented voice was quivering, sounding suddenly her real age of around twenty. 'For this I will kill you!' The door slammed shut, and Susie smiled tiredly at the venomous way the bolts slammed home outside. That Senta was capable of carrying out her threat was quite possible, but she wasn't afraid. She curled up on the bed again. Senta had been so furious that she hadn't even noticed the radio. She touched it. Tangible evidence of her conspiracy with Comrade Wolf. Conspiracy of a secret kindness that had abruptly flared into passion.

Susie closed her eyes, thinking of her father. It seemed to have been so long since she'd seen his face that it was almost difficult getting it into focus. . . .

She was alone for a long time after that. The hours seemed to stretch infinitely. She slept intermittently, dreaming vividly of Wolf. Keeping time by the radio, she realised that her keepers had missed at least one mealtime. Hunger started gnawing inside her, becoming a sharp pang, and she began to get uneasy. Was this her punishment for attacking Wolf? Or had they simply forgotten about her? It was hard not to panic at the thought that she might be left to die down here, starved like an animal.

She husbanded her water carefully, eking out each mouthful she took. Her thirst seemed exaggerated by hunger—and the fear that had now returned. Violence didn't frighten her now. Dying of hunger in this kennel did.

And then, carelessly pacing, she knocked the jug over. The precious fluid spilled across the floor before she could right it, and she felt a cold shiver up her spine. She ran to the door, and banged her fist against it.

'Wolf! Wolf!' Her voice was dry in her throat. There was no sound from beyond the grey door.

'*Wolf,*' she sobbed, 'Don't leave me like this. . . .'
Gradually, she pulled herself together, and walked
slowly back to the bed. There was no use in using
up her energy like this. She simply had to wait.

She curled up under the blankets, and prayed
for sleep.

When next she woke, the radio told her that it
was late afternoon. Over twenty-four hours had
passed since the last time her door had been
opened. She was now seriously hungry, and her
throat was dry.

'Wolf,' she whispered. 'For God's sake, what
are you doing to me?' She raised her head as a
sound came from behind the door. Relief surged
through her, warming her. Someone had come at
last. She sat up on the bed, praying it would be
Wolf. She needed the comfort of his arms right
now.

The bolts clattered, and the door swung open.
Two complete strangers stared in at her, middle-
aged men in black uniforms with black caps.
Susie's eyes widened in incredulity.

'Who are *you*?' she blinked, as if in a dream.

'Miss Susan Cheyne?'

She nodded, and slid to the edge of the bed,
beginning to tremble. The older of the two men,
his round, kindly face sporting a large moustache,
came over to her, reaching for her arms. 'Be calm
now.' His accent was heavily Italian. 'We've
arrested Alba Rossa, all of them. You're all right.'

'Who are you?' she repeated numbly.

'State police,' the other man smiled. 'It's all
over, Miss Cheyne——'

'The police?' she repeated. Uneasily, she thrust
aside the man's attempt to help her up. Her mind
was struggling to assimilate their presence here.

She knew it was insane, but her gut-reaction was one of hostility.

The question that had been thrusting against her consciousness suddenly burst out on her lips.

'Wolf,' she said sharply, studying their faces. 'Have you caught Wolf?' The policemen looked at each other in surprise. A policewoman joined them at the door, her face breaking into a delighted smile as she caught sight of Susie. 'Wolf,' she repeated, her body rigid. 'A tall man, dark hair, green eyes. Where is he?'

'No one of that name has been detained,' the second policeman said, looking puzzled. 'There was no one of that description in the gang.' Relief was sharp enough to make her gasp. So he was free! As though speaking to a child, he went on, 'We are the police, Miss Cheyne. We've been looking for you throughout the length and breadth of Italy. You're safe now!'

Susie stared at him, her numbness beginning to give way to the joy of total relief.

'You'll be with your father within hours,' he promised, taking her arm and leading her to the door. 'Your abductors are all in custody.'

The policewoman examined her carefully.

'Are you hurt, *signorina*? You look as though someone has been ill-treating you.'

Suddenly, she flung her arms round the woman's neck, laughing through her tears.

'I'm all right,' she told the now-beaming faces weepily. 'Bless you, bless you all! I'm all right. . . .'

Celebrity was an ordeal that began as soon as she stepped out of the farmhouse door, and confronted the mass of police Fiats, ambulances, flashing lights, and uniformed men outside. The cheer that went up as she appeared was almost as frightening as it was exhilarating; after the solitude of her cell, the sight of so many people was a little overwhelming. The press didn't seem to have arrived, but she knew they wouldn't be long.

The policewoman, close at her side, was murmuring in her ear, 'A very quick visit to the doctors, just for a check-up, and then you'll be joining your father, probably in Milan.'

'Where are we?' she asked, flinching as police cameras flashed, recording the event.

'Lombardia,' the policewoman informed her as they walked her through the crowd towards the ambulance. 'North-west Italy. Alitalia are going to arrange a special flight for your father to come and meet you.'

'*Signorina!*' The first reporter, sharper-nosed than his colleagues, had just arrived on the scene, and had the excitement of a scoop in his bespectacled eyes. He tried to keep pace beside the burly policemen, his notebook at the ready. 'How does it feel to be free?'

'I just want to see my father,' she said shakily. A policeman elbowed him aside, and she heard the reporter asking him, 'Did they do anything to her? Torture?' His voice was drowned out by the sudden roar of a police helicopter swooping overhead. Its rotors buffeted the earth into dusty uproar, the late afternoon sun dazzling in the clouds.

She was shaking as they put her in the back of the ambulance. She could hear the siren start up on the roof above. So many strangers, so much noise! She'd have given anything to have had Wolf's strong arms around her. The irony of it made her laugh slightly hysterically. Again, as at the very beginning of her kidnapping, she had the crazy sense that this was all a film, in which she was a central character.

The policewoman climbed in after her, as did the moustached policeman. She had just noticed the ribbons and badges that glittered on his uniform; he was evidently a very senior officer.

The two paramedics who'd been waiting for her insisted that she lie on the stretcher, and they covered her with a beautifully soft blanket. Fingers tested her pulse, reminding her sharply of Wolf. His freedom was one of the most important things in her mind right now. The doors slammed shut, closing off the worst of the noise, and several concerned faces stooped over her as the ambulance set off. It was like being a child again, sick in bed with measles, surrounded by solemn grown-ups.

'How did you find me?' she asked.

'One of the gang informed,' the senior officer told her. 'You mentioned someone called Wolf, Miss Cheyne.'

'Yes,' she nodded. 'He was the leader.'

'So?' Again, glances were exchanged. 'We shall want to hear more about this Wolf, when you're feeling up to it.'

'When can I see my father?' she begged. The senior officer's face broke into a compassionate smile.

'Your father was only informed of your discovery a few minutes ago. He does not know even whether you are alive or dead,' he informed her. 'I think you can give him that news yourself, don't you?' Her eyes gave him all the answer he needed. He lifted the receiver off its bracket against the bulkhead, and spoke into it rapidly. Everyone was smiling. With odd clarity, she thought what an odd scene she must make—a scruffy, dirty, blonde in jeans, surrounded by immaculate police officers. She giggled again—but she was still crying softly. Minutes later, he passed the receiver to her, and she clutched it to her ear.

'Daddy?'

'Susie!' She heard his voice cracking, like something that had been strained a long time, and was finally giving way. 'Are you all right?'

'I'm fine,' she said, laughing through her tears again. 'Absolutely fine!'

'Did they hurt you?' he asked, not bothering to conceal the fact that he was crying, too.

'No! They just kept me locked up. Oh, Dad! You must have been out of your mind all these weeks!'

'Where are you?' he demanded.

'I don't know. Somewhere in Lombardy. I've been kept in the cellar of a farmhouse——'

'The *bastards*,' he grated, his voice shaking with anger. 'It was all my fault.'

'Dad! Don't you dare say that!'

'It was my fault, for not taking good enough care of you, Susie.' She heard him blow his nose. 'We're going to set that right, my love. I've taken you for granted for too long now. We're going to be father and daughter again, I swear it.'

'I can't wait to see you,' she smiled weakly. 'Oh, Dad, they're going to fly you to Milan to meet me tonight. Isn't that wonderful?'

'Susie, I—I can't believe it. It's like a dream!' He suddenly sounded old to her, his voice frail. She closed her eyes, imagining what he must have gone through. He'd been so strong in the aftermath of her mother's death—but this must have been worse, worse because of the uncertainty.

'You must believe it,' she said, forcing herself to be strong, for his sake. 'I'm free, Dad. It's all over, for ever.'

CHAPTER EIGHT

THE elephant's trunk, graceful as a ballerina's arm, reached towards the paper bag Susie was holding out for him. She watched his wrinkled eyes, elephant-calm and elephant-wise, blinking gently as the delicate tip fossicked in the bag for the last monkey-nut, hoovered it up, and curled back to pop the tiny morsel into his huge pink mouth.

'Wouldn't think he'd even taste that, would you, Miss?' the keeper grinned.

'I think he only takes them to please me,' Susie admitted. She knew for a fact that Alfie preferred sticky buns, but she liked to vary his treat. 'Goodbye, Alfie.' She leaned over the rail to pat Alfie's powerful old trunk. That, too, was a tiny gesture—but Alfie's rumble of pleasure showed that it had been appreciated as much as the monkey-nuts. It was a great privilege to be allowed to feed Alfie titbits, and Susie gave the keeper a special smile as she walked out into the main concourse of the Zoo.

She'd been coming here as often as she could while she was in London, writing up her report at the Geophysical Institute nearby; since a childhood visit to Whipsnade, she'd always had a weakness for Zoos—and particularly for the elephants in them!

It was second nature already for her to pause, giving the Special Branch policeman time to fall into step behind her. Brown-Shoes was on duty today, one of the tougher-looking guards she'd had.

More than six weeks after her release from the farmhouse, the police were still keeping an eye on her. She hadn't argued; after her release she'd been desperately insecure, and even going out into the street had been terrifying. She'd insisted on resuming her normal life completely, knowing that the only way to combat her fear was to face it; but they'd stressed the need to be vigilant, at least for a few weeks more.

Wolf, after all, was still at large, even though the rest of the Alba Rossa cell were safely behind bars.

The police bodyguards had given her a wonderful sense of comfort at first, but by now they were growing slightly oppressive—evidence of how far she'd recovered from her ordeal.

She paused again at the taxi-rank, waiting for Brown-Shoes to arrange his own taxi, just behind hers. Brown-shoes was a tough-looking character in his late thirties, who reminded Susie of Karl Malden in his hey-day. He knew where she would be going—she always gave them a schedule of her movements for each day.

'Harley Street, please,' she told the cab-driver. Today was her last appointment with Dr Anthony Welch, the psychiatrist who'd been examining her since her return from Switzerland to resume her normal life, four weeks ago. There had been remarkably few serious emotional after-effects of the experience, he'd emphasised, but at her father's request he'd been monitoring her progress.

Once in the consulting-rooms, Brown-Shoes took up his position next to the potted palm in the plush waiting-room. He was already exchanging meaningful looks with the highly pneumatic

Miss Brownjohn at Reception while Susie went in to face Dr Welch for the last time.

This time he ushered her to the padded seat in front of his desk. Emotional balance, she'd noted with dry amusement, could be measured in terms of horizontality; when she'd first arrived, he'd made her lie flat on the couch. She'd progressed through the chaise longue, the sofa, and the armchair to this final summit—being trusted to sit upright.

'You look wonderful,' the psychiatrist said complacently, as though he'd just painted her himself. And, apart from the fact that her hair was an odd two-tone of raven and blonde that punks on the Edgware Road thought was madly fashionable, she *was* looking well. Her skin had regained its bloom, and her angular lines, she was sad to see, were giving way to lush curves again. Against her tanned skin, the heavy gold bracelet— her father's way of telling her how glad he'd been to see her again—gleamed seductively. 'How's your report going?'

'I'll finish it this week-end,' she told him. 'There's just an Index to write up, and it'll be done.' He was still waiting, so she went on, 'Getting back to work after nearly three weeks' enforced idleness has been wonderful, Doctor. You can't imagine how stimulating it is.'

'The report's due to be tabled in a week's time, isn't it?'

She nodded. 'I'm crossing my fingers that the Government will appoint a committee to examine the problems of seashore pollution in more detail. I've just skimmed the surface.' She smiled rather self-consciously. 'I've made some fairly radical recommendations, including the suggestion that hot water from nuclear power-stations should be re-used for secondary industry, or *anything*, rather than conveniently pumped into the sea—and that isn't going to be popular in certain quarters.'

'You'll survive.' Dr Welch steepled his thin hands, closing his eyes to summon concentration. 'Susan, I want to use this last meeting to go back over some of the ground we've covered over the past four weeks. Yes?'

'Go ahead,' Susie invited.

'Right, then. Let's consider your involvement with the man called Wolf.'

'Yes,' Susie said, seeing a pair of deep, vivid green eyes in her mind. The inner tensions she'd become so good at hiding clenched inside her mind. Where was he now, the man called Wolf? Hiding? Walking the streets of some great city, free and proud?

'We've got Wolf into perspective now,' Dr Welch observed, his eyes still painfully closed, rather like a vicar Susie had once known, who'd adopted the same mannerism even when saying the most banal things. She remembered seeing that martyred, saintly expression on his face as he'd complimented her mother on a batch of scones (Really *very* good, Mrs Cheyne, very good *indeed*). 'We've learned that infatuations between kidnapper and kidnappee are not uncommon. You are not to be blamed if, during the course of your ordeal, you invested this man with a degree of authority—even affection—which he did not merit. We've accepted that.' Susie nodded, unable to keep a wry smile off her mouth. Dr Welch always said 'we' when he meant 'you'. 'We've also accepted that Wolf, no matter how——' Dr Welch opened his eyes at last '—*attractive* a man he might be, is also a very dangerous and wicked man. So dangerous that the police were scarcely aware of his existence until they heard your evidence.' He pulled his notepad towards him, and pointed his thin, ascetic face at Susie like a radar screen. 'You no longer dream about him, do you, Susan?'

'Never,' Susie lied. She dreamed about him every second night, achingly confused dreams of fear and longing. She couldn't share those dreams with Dr Welch. Though they left her sweating and disturbed, they were far too precious to lose. They were all she had left of Wolf; and each time she saw him and touched him in her dreams was a bright moment of passion snatched from the past.

'How *do* you feel about Wolf now?' he probed, watching her. She felt tightness clench her throat-muscles. What she felt, above all, was a blind anger. Anger that he'd made her need him so badly, and had then left her forever.

Except she couldn't tell that to Dr Welch, who would inevitably pass the information on to her father.

'I'm not really bothered about him any more,' she answered. 'As you've just said, he's a wicked man. I was almost obsessed with him for a while—but I've long since got over that.'

It was a lie. And yet she really *did* want to believe Dr Welch, and feel that Wolf was out of her system for ever. Wolf was a killer, a terrorist. Even now he could be planning to kill or kidnap again. And one day he would meet his destiny in some back-alley shoot-out. She bit her lip, hard. She did want to believe Dr Welch. Believing wasn't enough, though. She simply didn't *want* him out of her system, no matter how fiercely her mind might reject him.

And she hadn't told anyone, not Welch, nor the police, nor her father, that her feelings for Wolf went beyond infatuation. That he'd made love to her. She'd once believed—no, *prayed*—that what she'd come to feel for Wolf was a kind of madness that would pass away once she was free. But over the past weeks it had become increasingly obvious to her, despite her strenuous efforts to fool herself, her father, and Dr Welch, that she'd seriously underestimated the force of her own emotions.

Her feelings about Wolf hadn't changed. But *she* had changed. From the girl she'd been when she'd left for Zurich a few short months ago, she was now a woman. Anguish and tension had helped do that. But what had done it most of all was the emotions that Wolf had made her feel—emotions that simply weren't going to be psychoanalysed away.

'. . . so you seem to have recovered remarkably well from the whole experience,' the psychiatrist was saying, and she switched her wandering attention back to him, glad to be off the subject of Wolf for the time being. It frightened her.

'Now. Your father had always been a distant man, before the kidnapping. You told me——' He consulted his notes. 'You told me you always felt you could get closer to him. When you first started coming to these sessions you said that the best thing that had come out of the kidnapping had been a *rapprochement* between you and your father. You felt that he was closer to you than he had been for some years. Do you still feel that?'

'More than ever,' Susie nodded. 'He telephones me two or three times a week now. We're a family again, even though there are just the two of us. He'll never be a *warm* person—that just isn't in him. But he went through a bad time, especially when the negotiations seemed to be breaking down. Two million pounds was an incredible sum to ask—my father didn't have anything like that amount, and there were times when he really thought he'd lost me.'

'Things could have turned out badly,' the psychiatrist agreed. 'It was lucky that one of the gang gave the police a tip-off. What was his name?'

'Draco,' she replied, remembering the pig-like face all too well. It was ironic to think that she owed her freedom, maybe her life as well, to the man who'd tried to rape her. Evidently, though, Draco's defeat at Wolf's hands had rankled bitterly enough for him to give the whole game away to the police. 'Anyway, it's brought Dad and me together, which is a wonderful thing.'

'Excellent,' Dr Welch repeated. 'That you can find good things about the experience shows how well you've adjusted.' He tapped his pen gently on the notepad. 'And things are going well between you and young Dr Dowson?'

'We get along fine,' Susie nodded. Which was only partly true; since she'd come back from Zurich there had been a gap between her and Joe that would never be bridged, and they both knew it, deep down, though they'd been trying hard to ignore it.

'Any physical contact?'

Susie flushed slightly, but met the psychiatrist's eyes steadily. Her father was paying a lot of money for these consultations, and she felt guilty about fobbing the doctor off with so many half-truths and white lies. 'We kiss and cuddle, Doctor. But we're not—sleeping together.'

'Is that because you prefer it that way?'

'Yes,' she admitted, still slightly pink. Not that Joe had ever pushed her in any way, but she knew he wanted her, and she knew he believed that making love might dissolve that unspoken barrier between them. 'Joe's very kind,' she told him. 'And very understanding. I just don't feel that I'm ready for that yet.'

'And yet you've told me that you're not a virgin?'

'That's right.' Now her flush was hot and spreading. To explain her non-virginity she'd told Welch that she'd had a short affair with a man in Canada, and he had no idea that her single, unforgettable, experience of making love had been on a wild Lombardy hillside—with Comrade Wolf.

'Hmmm.' He made a note, donning half-rimmed spectacles to do so. 'You know,' he advised, not looking up at her as he wrote, 'it's about time you resumed a good, healthy relationship again, Susan. You're twenty-two, and very attractive. I'm sure you know what I mean. No religious scruples about that sort of thing, I trust?'

'Well—no,' Susie hesitated. Dr Welch, despite his vicar-like appearance, was a free-thinking humanist, and it occasionally startled her to hear him come out with advice like this. 'Not exactly. But I wouldn't want to embark on a physical relationship with a man I didn't love. I mean, I'd have to be completely sure about my feelings for him before I jumped into bed with him.' Indeed, her heart asked her drily. You were as confused as hell when you let Wolf take you!

'Ah.' He permitted himself one of his rare smiles. 'I wouldn't let that worry you too much. There's nothing wrong with sex, after all. We surround it with too many taboos and regulations. We all need it, you know. The man next door needs it. You need it. I need it.' His eyes wandered vaguely round the room as he removed his spectacles. 'Miss Brownjohn at Reception needs it. . . .' He lapsed into a trance-like silence, as though contemplating the glory of Miss Brownjohn's highly pneumatic needs. She had to bite back a smile.

'So,' Dr Welch said, coming to life again, and slipping his spectacles back on his thin nose, 'you get cracking, my girl. If Dr Dowson's not up to it, find someone who is. You'll thank me for the advice.'

Ten minutes later, she was hurrying along Wigmore Street to keep her lunch-appointment with Joe, still smiling at the psychiatrist's serious advice. *Go out and get laid.* Was that the twentieth-century panacea to all ills? Anyway, at least she didn't have to face any more appointments with Dr Welch. Her report was almost completed, she had a sheaf of job-offers for the winter to go through and, all in all, she had every right to be a very happy young woman on this early October morning.

And if she tried really hard, she could almost believe that she was.

Joe was already waiting at Gaspard's, looking cuddly, but not exactly good-tempered, in his woolly black beard. He shot Brown-Shoes an irritable glance as he rose to kiss Susie hullo.

'I'm getting rather sick of these goons in attendance all the time,' he said as they sat down.

'Brown-Shoes isn't a goon,' she reproved. 'He's only doing his job, and I'm sure it's a very boring one.' She covered his hand, smiling into the brown eyes. 'What's upset you like this?'

'Fairbourne,' he grimaced. 'Something's come up at the research station, and I have to get back there this afternoon.'

'Oh, hell,' she sighed. He'd arranged a special week-end off to be with her in London, and she felt his disappointment keenly.

'I don't suppose you could travel back up with me on the train——?' he suggested.

'My report,' she said unhappily. 'I *have* to get it done by Monday, Joe—and all my notes are at the Institute or the flat. . . .'

'Yes.' He offered her a slightly twisted smile. 'I forgot. There's always something coming between us, isn't there?'

'I wouldn't say that.' She waited as the waiter came to take their order, noticing that Brown-Shoes, a few tables away, was just having a glass of water. Police salaries didn't stretch to lunches in restaurants, and he'd be turning to his bag of sandwiches sometime in the afternoon. Was there a Mrs Brown-Shoes somewhere, who made him spam and chutney sandwiches? A Mrs Brown-Shoes whose life would be wrecked for ever if someone like Comrade Wolf were to put a bullet in Brown-Shoes's heart?

'What *would* you say, then?' Joe asked, cutting into her thoughts.

'I'd say we both had jobs that needed a lot of attention,' she replied mildly. In a way it was a relief to have so many excuses—like work—to blame for the lukewarmness of their relationship. Lukewarm on her part, anyway. A pang of compassion stung her. Poor Joe! He had a lot to contend with. 'But I'll be free once the report's done,' she went on gently. 'And you've got leave coming up later this month, Joe. Hey,' she said persuasively, kissing his cheek, 'let's take a break somewhere then. Wales, or maybe Scotland. Just the two of us.'

'Just the three of us,' he corrected drily. 'You, me, and the Special Branch.'

'I've never known you so grumpy,' she smiled. 'They obviously think it's worth keeping an eye on me, or they wouldn't bother. And Wolf still hasn't been captured.'

Joe shrugged, obviously discontented. That was one of the things that kept them apart. She'd seen the violent side of life, and he hadn't. He hadn't been kept in a cell for three weeks, and would never really believe that the police guards were anything more than a nuisance. Her whole ordeal was somehow unreal to him, like something from a thriller.

His resentment about the Special Branch men, Dr Welch, or any references to her ordeal was, she knew, a kind of jealousy. Not simply jealousy of Wolf, but jealousy that stemmed from his understanding that something had happened to her in those weeks which had put a barrier between them for ever.

He didn't refer to her idea of a holiday together, and she didn't press the point. They ate for a few minutes.

'Sometimes,' he said wrily, looking up at her at last, 'I think Comrade Wolf is more real to you than I am.'

'That's silly,' she said sharply.

'Is it? What do you think about when you go into those trances, Susie? Like just now?'

'I certainly don't think about Wolf,' she retorted. 'Wolf was a murderer, a criminal, Joe. You're crazy to be jealous of him.'

'Crazy,' he repeated. He fished in the pocket of his tweed jacket for a tartan handkerchief, and polished his glasses prior to putting them on. 'Remember that afternoon we spent on the river last week?'

'Yes,' she nodded in puzzlement.

'We hired a punt, and had a picnic on the water, and you fell asleep on the cushions.'

'Yes,' she said again, remembering the afternoon as an idyllic one, of swans and peaceful reflections on the Thames.

'You were calling his name out in your sleep. Wolf's name.'

He picked up his knife and fork, and addressed himself to his steak again. Susie sat in a chilled silence, watching him. The waiter, passing by, paused with a worried look.

'Anything wrong with your spaghetti, madame?'

'No,' she said, forcing a gay smile, 'it's delicious—thank you.'

'So,' Joe said as the waiter moved off. 'What do you say to that?'

'Joe,' she said quietly, feeling desperately sorry for him, 'that was a very vivid experience in my life. Wolf terrified me most of the time. And after I was released, the police questioned me about him for days and days—what did he look like, what nationality did I think he was, what identifying marks did he have——' She broke off, re-living those debriefing sessions in zurich. Nothing had interested them as much as Comrade Wolf, the unknown enemy. 'He hadn't been on their files, you see, and they wanted to know every tiny detail

about him, especially when they heard he'd killed
Johann Weiss. I can't help it if I have nightmares
about him from time to time.'

'This wasn't a nightmare,' he interrupted. 'And
your voice wasn't frightened. It was something
else.'

She didn't have to ask him what. She pushed her
plate away, her appetite gone, and toyed with her
wine-glass, her deep blue eyes suddenly dark.

'Why didn't you tell me he'd made love to you?'
Joe asked, almost conversationally.

The colour drained from Susie's cheeks as she
felt her heart shrivel inside her.

'I know this isn't a lunch-time subject,' he went
on, not looking at her. 'I'd wanted to bring this up
over the week-end, but we don't have the time any
more now.'

'What is it you want, Joe?' she asked, feeling
cold all over, and wishing to hell she could avoid
this conversation.

'I want the truth,' he said firmly.

'The truth,' she repeated. What was the truth?
That she was hopelessly in love with Wolf, would
always be in love with him? What crumbs of hope
could she offer Joe, who had once seemed so
wonderful to her, but who could never now take
the place of Wolf in her heart? 'All right.' She
tasted the dry wine, realising that no more white
lies were going to do now. 'I didn't tell you about
it for the same reasons I didn't tell my father,' she
said quietly.

'Try me,' he invited, watching her through his
gold-rimmed spectacles.

'Firstly,' she said, taking a deep breath, 'because
I don't think you'd ever understand. I don't
necessarily understand it myself.' *That* was the

literal truth. 'And secondly, because I didn't want to hurt you.'

'Is there a thirdly?' he enquired, his face a little paler now that the truth he'd wanted was coming out.

'Yes,' she nodded, 'and you won't like it. Thirdly, because it was none of your business.'

'It's my business now,' he contradicted her. His mouth was bitter. 'I don't need to ask whether you enjoyed it.'

'That's not fair,' she said, the colour draining from her cheeks. She'd known that he'd never understand, and she didn't feel in the mood to justify or excuse herself, either. Sickness made her press her fists into her eyes.

'Just answer one question,' he said. Brown-Shoes was watching them curiously across the restaurant, clearly aware from their expressions that all was not well between them. 'Did he take advantage of you—or did you consent to his lovemaking?'

'You make it sound horrible,' she shuddered. That terrible, wonderful morning in the sun rose up so sharply in her mind that she could smell the crushed thyme in her nostrils, remember the song of the birds. 'There just isn't an answer to those questions, Joe. It isn't like some scientific problem, clean-cut and analysable. I'm really very sorry you found out. I didn't want you to know, not ever.'

'I find it very hard to understand how you could——' he tried to control his expression, but revulsion was written plainly in his face '—could make love to someone like that.'

'I'll tell you something else I've never told anyone,' she said, answering the accusation indirectly, and trying not to let his predictable reaction hurt her. 'I also tried to kill Wolf.'

'*You?*'

'Me.' She stared into the blood-red wine. 'I tried to throttle him, and damn-near got myself killed in the process.' He was staring at her in shock. 'People do things like that when they're under stress,' she said quietly. 'Even your sweet little Susan. I found out a lot about myself during those three weeks, Joe. I can't ask you to understand. But I can—and do—ask you to try and forgive.'

'I'd forgive you anything.' He stared at the sweet oval face, the deep blue eyes and full mouth so exotically set off by the glossy raven hair that was growing back after its peroxide bleach. 'I love you, Susie.'

It was the first time he'd said it so directly, and she reached for his hand, knowing that her reaction was more of pity than returned love. He took it, studying her long, slender fingers almost absently. She couldn't help thinking of the way she'd tried to strangle Wolf, and her terrible, heart-rending remorse afterwards.

'I know you don't love me. No—let me have my say. It'll only take a second. All I have is the hope that you will, some day. I'm going to try my damnedest to *make* you love me! And I hope that one day you'll tell me about Wolf. Try and make me understand.'

She nodded, feeling a lump in her throat. There was something so gentle about Joe, so honest. But would she ever feel anything more than compassion for him? If it hadn't been for Wolf, she knew, she could well have come back from her holiday and married this man. They were so suited in so many ways, in their mutual interests as well as emotionally.

But now? She was carrying out the appearance of a relationship with Joe, really trying quite hard to fall in love with him—and yet it simply wasn't working. It was becoming little more than a charade, carried out for God knew what benefit. . . . It might be a lot kinder to just wrench herself away from Joe and the security he represented, and let him get over her in peace.

'There isn't room in your life for two men,' he pointed out, echoing her thoughts. 'I don't know anything about this Wolf, and you're right in telling me it's none of my business.' He leaned over earnestly. 'But you can never have him, Susie. He's on the other side of the tracks. Permanently. There would be no chance of a marriage, of children, a life together, even if you *did* ever see him again. And I think you know by now that I'm offering you all those things.'

'I'm deeply honoured,' Susie said in a low voice. 'That means a great deal to me, Joe.'

'I'm going back to Fairbourne on the 3.30,' he said, his voice lighter now. She suddenly felt a rush of affection for the delicate way he'd put everything. 'Good luck with your report, Susie. Think about what I've said. Maybe,' he added softly, 'once we've got Comrade Wolf out of the way, you and I will be able to reach each other at last.'

'I'd like nothing better, Joe.' She was holding both his hands now, trying to fight down her inclination to cry. She wasn't going to meet anyone more sincere or kind than Joe, not ever. 'But I'm not worthy of you. I'm really not.' She'd put on such a brave show for Dr Welch this morning—but the real truth was that she was confused, deeply and painfully so. Confused about everything except one overwhelming fact—that beside Wolf, no other man could ever possess her heart. They might touch it, the way Joe did. But she could never be completely committed to anyone else.

Not until, as he'd said, Comrade Wolf was out of the way. And that might never be.

'Here,' he said, mock-solemn, 'you let me be the judge of your worthiness, okay?'

'Okay,' she said. 'You're a good man, Joe Dowson.'

She threw herself into her work with such determination that afternoon that by six-thirty the Index was finished. With a strong sense of triumph, she surveyed the 200-page document in front of her: *Industry, Power and The Sea: A Report on Coastal Pollution in Britain*, by Susan Cheyne, MSc.

Gleefully, she scooped up the hefty file, and set off home at such a smart pace that Brown-Shoes was almost left behind.

'In a hurry, Miss Cheyne?' he asked as they walked down the corridor.

'Not really,' she grinned. 'I've just finished my report, that's all.'

'Great,' he said in satisfaction.

'I didn't know you were so interested in my work,' she said.

'Frankly, I'm not.' He surveyed the hallowed halls of the Institute. 'But I wasn't half getting sick of sitting around in *this* place all day, I'll tell you that!'

She was still chuckling when she got back home to Islington. She 'phoned her father after eight to give him the good news, and they had a warm,

amused conversation. He was still the same old
Dad, intent on his career and on the material
world; but there was a closeness between them
now—what had Welch called it? A *rapprochement*.
And that was worth rubies.

She also tried to 'phone Joe, to tell him she'd be
able to make it to Fairbourne this week-end after
all, but he wasn't answering his 'phone. He was
probably still at the Institute. Never mind, she'd
surprise him by just arriving tomorrow morning!

At eight-thirty the doorbell rang. It was the next
Special Branch man, taking over from Brown-
Shoes.

'Everything all right, Miss Cheyne?'

'Yes, fine,' she smiled. 'Can I make you a cup of
coffee? Cocoa?'

'Don't bother—I'll be fine.' He was another
burly man, reassuringly broad and tall. 'Just you
lock up securely, and use the buzzer if you've got
the slightest doubt about *anything*.'

'Okay,' she nodded. 'Goodnight.'

'Goodnight, Miss Cheyne.' She latched the
door, not envying him his night in the front seat of
the Rover parked outside her flat. She was deeply
grateful for the care they were taking of her, even
if it was slightly oppressive at times. There wasn't
a back entrance to the flat, which was near
enough to the Arsenal Football Stadium to be
deafening on match-days, and she didn't fancy
anyone's chances of getting past the Special
Branch man in his Rover.

She watched a little television, read *The
Standard*, and simply gloated over her finished
report. By eleven she was ready for bed. On the
bedside table, within easy reach, was the buzzer
they'd given her. She simply had to press the

button to bring help hurtling up to the flat. She'd been in mortal dread of setting it off accidentally— say while groping for a glass of water in the night.

She undressed, thinking of the conversation she'd had with Joe at lunch. He really did love her, she believed that. It was an odd thought to know that, whenever she wanted, he would marry her. Just like that. There was a capacity of gentleness in him which attracted her strongly towards him. He was soothing, kind, and many women had been glad to marry for less qualities than those. Whether they were enough to hold her, though, remained to be seen. She prayed so.

She pulled on shortie pyjamas in deference to October, and was just about to climb into bed with the latest Len Deighton when she heard the front door click shut.

It was a sound that froze her, making her hair stand up on the back of her neck. She'd latched it—hadn't she? Or had she forgotten? There was a silence. She glanced at the buzzer, picked it up instinctively, and walked nervously into the living room with it, her thumb on the button.

She'd left a single standard-lamp glowing softly, the way she always did.

Wolf was standing in the middle of the room.

CHAPTER NINE

HER gasp was almost a sob. He watched her with eyes narrowed to green slits, that faint, mocking smile etched on his mouth. He was still holding the skeleton key with which he'd opened her door.

'Well?' He indicated the emergency buzzer in her hands. 'Are you going to set the dogs on me, Susie?'

She stood paralysed. The memory of that grey prison swept through her mind. Memories of fear and violence, and a morning of shuddering passion in the grass. Then, as though something had snapped inside her, her fingers opened nervelessly, and she dropped the buzzer on to the carpet at her feet.

He was with her in a second, arms drawing her tight against the lean hardness of his body. She clung to him, her fingers digging almost desperately into the muscles of his shoulders. Nothing mattered any more, only this consuming need she felt for him. She was shaking uncontrollably as he kissed her temples and eyelids with fierce tenderness. The scrape of his man's chin against her soft skin brought back vivid memories of the last time they'd touched.

'You smell so good,' he said huskily, smiling at her with eyes that were veiled with thick, dark lashes. He kissed her mouth, hard. Her lips were almost too shocked to respond.

'*God damn you,*' she whispered unevenly, still unable to believe that this was really happening,

'what are you doing here? Don't you know there
are police outside?'

'I couldn't stay away.' He stepped back to pull
off the neutral grey bomber-jacket, and tossed it
on to the couch. He was looking tired, and the
denims and black polo-neck he wore were creased,
as though he'd slept in them.

Feeling that her legs weren't going to support
her much longer, Susie sank on to a chair, her
hands clasped between her bare knees, and stared
up at him. 'Oh, sweet Lord,' she said numbly.
'They'll kill you!'

'They'll have to catch me first,' he observed
drily. She watched the achingly familiar line of his
body as he moved to the window, and looked
carefully through the gap between the curtain and
the wall. 'Just the man in the Rover?'

She nodded silently. Her heart was pounding
hard, her mouth dry as a bone.

'What have you come for?' she asked fearfully.
'To take me away again?'

He glanced at her, his tanned face wearing an
odd expression.

'No,' he said with surprising gentleness. 'This is
a social call, Susie. I came to see you.' The buzzer
was still lying on the floor, and her eyes were
dragged towards it. Turmoil was rife inside her.
Logic told her to snatch it up and press it, accuse
him as the man who'd kept her in lonely
confinement for three weeks, torturing her father's
nerves without remorse. He followed her eyes.

'I'm not armed,' he said obliquely. 'I wouldn't
be able to put up much of a fight if that watch-dog
out there were to come bursting in with his
cannon.' He ran his fingers wearily through his
close-cropped dark hair. 'To tell you the truth, I

might even be glad to give it all up, and get some rest. . . .'

She didn't move. A phrase of Dr Welch's was echoing weirdly through her mind. *Infatuations between kidnapper and kidnappee are not uncommon.* What spell was it he cast over her? He came over to her, and gathered her in his arms again. She felt the hard muscles under the soft wool of his sweater. And on the tanned column of his neck she could see a faint bruise. Her mark.

Her lips were parted to receive his kiss. It was piercingly sweet, an act of gentleness that swelled into desire. His hands caressed her body hungrily through the cotton of her pyjamas as she clung to him.

'You've put on weight,' he said roughly. 'You were half-starved at the farmhouse.'

'Wolf, Wolf. . . .' Tears seeped between her closed lids as he rocked her quietly in his arms. So many memories were flooding her mind, sharp and overwhelming. The mixture of grief and joy in her was hard to separate, each so strong and vivid.

'Are you all right?' he asked, brushing the hair away from her face. 'I learned that you've been seeing a psychiatrist twice a week.'

'I had my last appointment this morning,' she told him. The irony made her laugh with a touch of bitterness. 'He pronounced me a hundred percent fit. And now you have to come along!'

He studied her sharply for a few seconds, as though searching for something in her face. Then his frown eased. 'You'll survive,' he said, unconsciously echoing Dr Welch's words. 'You're as tough as old boots, Susan Cheyne.'

Feminine practicality restored itself somehow in

her mind. 'Are you hungry?' she asked, wiping her eyes and sitting up.

'Starving,' he nodded.

She searched through the flat's meagre store of provisions in her mind. 'I'll make you bacon and eggs,' she decided, getting up.

'Do you usually cook as late as this?' he queried.

'Sometimes,' she nodded. 'I often work late.'

'Watchdogs have sharp noses,' he explained, getting up and stretching his powerful arms. 'I wouldn't want your friend outside coming up to investigate the smell of sizzling bacon at eleven o'clock at night.'

'Clever Wolf,' she said drily, and fetched a dressing-gown to cover her minimal nightwear. The less bare skin she showed him, the more comfortable she was going to feel. She went into the kitchen, glad to have something to do with her trembling hands. This was aiding and abetting a criminal on the run, but she didn't care. It had come over her again, that feeling that there were just the two of them in the world. Things like right and wrong were irrelevant.

She suspected she'd never be able to betray him, no matter what he had done to her and her father. This was what it must feel like to be married to a criminal, to be forever torn between love and the law. Yet her anger against him was still very near the surface, ready to explode in a release of nervous tension. 'There must be something very wrong with my logic,' she muttered, half to herself. 'By rights I should put a tablespoon of arsenic in your damned eggs.'

He simply smiled, leaning against the fitted units to watch her. He was as hard-looking as ever, his body poised like an athlete's, even when at rest.

And there was the same lethal magnetism in the ruthless lines of his face. She'd described them so often to the police, drawn up a dozen Identikits— yet she'd never been able to capture the vitality in him, that glittering sense of life and power. She felt his clear tiger's eyes on her as she whisked eggs and dropped bacon into the hot pan, and turned her back on him determinedly. There were more flecks of grey at the dark temples than she'd remembered.

'Why are you in London, Wolf?' she asked quietly.

'To see you,' he replied calmly.

'Don't give me that,' she blurted, spinning to face him. 'You're just playing on my emotions, you pig!'

'Very well,' he shrugged, unimpressed by the way her temper had snapped. 'I had business in England. Not here, though. I made a special trip to see you.'

'Big deal,' she grated. *Business*. Sickened, she shook her head. 'More killing? Maybe blowing up a policeman? Or are you planning to snatch another rich man's daughter?'

'I have work to do,' he told her mildly, watching her with those vivid green eyes. 'I don't expect you to understand. I don't know whether I want you to.'

'Funny,' she said bitterly, 'I was saying exactly the same thing to someone else today.'

'Joe Dowson? Yes, I saw you giving him the True Confessions bit.'

She slammed the plate down, her anger rising like a lump in her chest. 'You mean you've been spying on me?' she asked in furious disbelief.

'That's an ugly word,' he smiled.

'Everything you do is ugly,' she told him venomously. Mockery sparkled in his laughter.

'If you think so. He asked you to marry him this morning, didn't he?'

She didn't trust herself to answer. Emotion was making her hands unsteady again as she sliced bread for him.

'Well?' he challenged. 'Are you going to accept him?'

'That's a bloody impertinent question!'

'I think it's a fair one.' His voice was cool. 'Is he your lover?'

'You stay out of my life,' she quivered, pointing the breadknife at him. 'You've done me enough damage to last a lifetime, Wolf. Joe's a good man, and he loves me. If you try to do anything to disrupt that, I'll—I'll kill you!'

'You don't love him.' The sentence was a statement, utterly, arrogantly confident. He picked up his plate, put it on the kitchen table, and sat down to eat. 'Have you got anything to drink?'

Wordlessly, she wrenched the fridge door open, and took out one of the cans of pale ale she kept there for Joe. He nodded thanks as she poured him a glass, and ate with the dedication of a very hungry man. Susie sat down slowly opposite him, trying to get a rein on her emotions. It was weird to think of the Special Branch man outside, placidly reading his Western while she sat here, facing one of the most dangerous men in Europe.

'Did the police give you a rough time after they found you?' he asked casually.

'They wanted to know all about *you*,' she told him, getting a mean satisfaction out of telling him that. 'They said they'd be hunting you high and low. I said I hoped they'd throw you in a dungeon for the rest of your life!'

'There's gratitude for you,' he observed through a mouthful of bacon.

'You were asking my father two million pounds for my release,' she accused. 'That was monstrous extortion!'

'I had nothing to do with the negotiations,' he told her flatly. 'The Executive Committee handled all that.'

'Yes,' she sneered. 'Funny that both you and your precious Executive Committee happen to be free—while all your stooges carry the can.'

'You mean Senta and the rest? I told you. Alba Rossa has to work with rotten materials.' His eyes glittered. 'Rotten materials are expendable, Susie.'

She watched him numbly as he drained half the beer in one slow long gulp. Did he have any feelings at all?

'What would you have done,' she asked, 'if my father hadn't been able to raise that kind of money? Would you have killed me?'

'That eventuality didn't arise,' he reminded her coolly. His indifference staggered her for a second. But she should have remembered—Wolf was an executive in the world of terror. It was all work to him. *Business*.

He finished eating in silence, and nodded yes to her offer of coffee.

'I like your flat,' he complimented, looking around the small, neat place she'd made.

'It's really only a base,' she told him grudgingly. 'I'm out in the field such a lot with my job. But I like it here. The rent's low, and it's cosy enough.' She glanced at him. 'Where are you staying?'

'Nowhere.' He stirred his coffee, his eyes taking

in the soft curve of her body under the gown she'd
wrapped round herself. 'I'm going to have to sleep
here tonight. Susie.'

'No.' Her heart was thudding suddenly. 'I won't
permit that, Wolf. You've got no right to involve
me in your plans——'

'Keep your voice down.' The command was like
a lash, for all it was softly spoken. Green leopard's
eyes raked hers. 'I'm not offering you a choice,
Susan. There are bigger things at stake here than
you could imagine.'

'But——'

'If you don't want me to stay, then call your
friend outside.' The challenge was point-blank. He
stood up. 'Thank you for the meal. I needed that. I
also need a wash and shave. Do you have a
shower?'

'There won't be much hot water at this time of
night,' she said inconsequentially, still trying to
grapple with the idea of his spending the night in
her flat.

'Any water will do.' He was already hauling
off his sweater as he walked through to the
bathroom, and she caught a glimpse of his
tanned back as he closed the door behind him.
There was a tired-looking bandage across his
lower ribs. He was hurt—hurt and on the run
Her quick sympathies leaped to him, and she sat
alone in the kitchen for a while, gnawing her
knuckles in desperation. What in God's name
was she to do? If she let him stay, she'd be
harbouring a man who might be on his way to
kill or injure innocent people.

Yet she couldn't turn him over to the police.
That would be unthinkable. They'd been lovers.
He'd protected her, in his twisted way, from

serious harm on more than one occasion. Now
was her turn to pay him back.

Ah, Comrade Wolf, she thought bitterly, you
drive a hard bargain.

Careful not to alert the Special Branch guard's
suspicion by showing too many lights, she found
spare blankets in a cupboard, and made him up a
bed as best she could on the sofa. He wasn't going
to be comfortable there, especially not if he was
badly hurt, but it would have to do. She could
hear the sound of the shower running, and she
hunted out the biggest towel she had. It was a little
mad, going through these hospitable motions on
behalf of Wolf. It occurred to her that if Joe ever
found out he'd spent the night with her, that
would be the end of their relationship.

Damn Wolf. He was six feet three inches of
sheer danger on the loose.

'Here's a towel,' she called through the
bathroom door. She hesitated. 'Do you want me
to wash any of your clothes?'

He switched off the shower, and opened the
door shamelessly to claim the towel—lithe, tanned,
and naked. 'You were right about the water. Have
you got an iron?'

'Y-yes,' she stammered, trying to keep her eyes
off his body.

'Could you press my jeans and jacket? They're
quite clean, but they're creased.' She nodded
blindly, turning away to get the Rowenta. 'What is
it?' he asked, amusement in his voice. 'You and I
don't have any secrets from each other, do we?'
She ignored the taunt, though her cheeks were
flaming, and set the ironing-board up in the
kitchen. Smooth, golden skin covering perfectly
developed muscles. The memory was seared into

her mind. His body had a mature power that would disturb the composure of a saint with sensual thoughts, and she was unsteady inside as she waited for the iron to heat up.

He came through, the towel wrapped like a sarong round his waist, and swivelled to show her the angry-looking scar across his ribs. It was only half-healed.

'I don't suppose you've got any bandages?' he asked.

'Only Elastoplast.' She pointed to the cupboard. 'There might be a roll of lint in there.' She pressed the clothes with over-intent care as he hunted for the lint. 'How did you do that?' she asked, trying to sound casual.

'I didn't do it,' he smiled drily. He didn't have to tell her it was a bullet-wound. He found what he wanted, and tore a strip of the right size. It was an awkward place, under his right arm, and she watched him struggling to get the lint over the wound for a minute. Then her compassion got the better of her, and she propped the iron up, and went over to him.

'Let me do this.' She examined the wound, relieved to see that it was quite clean. It obviously hadn't had medical treatment, though. She fixed the pad gently in place, and taped it on with Elastoplast. 'There.' Before she could back away, Wolf pulled her close with one arm, and ran his fingers through her two-tone hair with a wry smile.

'This looks crazy. Very Art Deco. You could start a Susie Cheyne look, black and white——' he studied her blush, '—and red all over.'

'Funny,' she snapped, pulling away. Her hair-colouring was as crazily mixed as her emotions, and she didn't care to be teased about it by the man who'd done it to her in the first place! 'I hope that *hurts*,' she said meaningfully, nodding at the snowy covering on his side.

'It's much better, thanks.' His sinewy torso gleamed in the light. 'I've left my other clothes on the radiator to dry—haven't you got a dressing-gown or something that would fit me?'

'I could lend you a nightie,' she said acidly, 'but it wouldn't fit.'

'Doesn't pal Joey leave a change of togs here?'

'Don't call him pal Joey,' she rasped. 'And no, he does *not* leave any clothes here!'

Dark brows arched over wickedly glinting green eyes.

'You don't mean to say you aren't living in sin?'

'You wouldn't understand anything else, would you?' she said, wondering why her scorn sounded so defensive.

'Well, well,' he mused. 'Looks like I was right about him, after all.'

She could cheerfully have slung the Rowenta at his head, but he was already moving off. She finished the ironing, cursing him under her breath, and switched it off. She hung his clothes over the back of the kitchen chair, and followed him—to find him calmly examining her bedroom.

'What do you have a double-bed for,' he asked, 'if you prefer sleeping alone?'

'I sleep diagonally,' she said sarcastically. The bed, which was a rather majestic Victorian affair in brass and enamel, had been a gift from her father when she'd first set up this flat, but she wasn't going to tell him that.

'Show me,' he invited, his eyes smoky. She felt her heart turn over at the desire she knew was in him, and had to moisten her dry lips.

'You're sleeping in the sitting room,' she informed him grimly.

'Indeed.' He picked up one of the pillows, touching the beautiful lace, and looked up at her. 'Belgian?'

'Yes.' Her one vanity had been to equip the bed with the sort of exquisite linen it would originally have had—frothy lace edgings and embroidered flowers. She took a shaky breath, trying to keep her eyes off his magnificent body. 'You're sleeping in the sitting room,' she repeated. 'Otherwise I *will* call the police!'

'I've missed you, Susie.' The huskily spoken words cut into her heart like a knife, and his eyes were holding hers with a depth of desire that made her weak. 'I risked my life to come here. And I didn't come to spend the night on the sofa.' He reached out, and switched the bedside lamp off. In the soft darkness, he came over to her, tugging the sash of her gown loose, and sliding it off her shoulders. 'Come to bed, Susie.'

'No,' she pleaded shakily. 'Don't do this to me, Wolf——' He took her hand, not answering, and drew her to the bed. Her nerves screamed a protest against what he was doing, what he was asking her to do. *'No,'* she moaned, trying to wrest her hand loose from his.

'I need you,' he said softly, pulling her down beside him. 'God, I need you so badly. . . .' His naked body was warm against her own, his hands sliding up under her pyjama-top to caress her back, tracing the graceful curve of her arched spine. Helplessly, she let him draw her close, her own arms finding their way around his neck. It was wrong, terribly wrong, but she was like a woman in a whirlpool, sucked irresistibly towards a vortex that was more powerful than her own will to resist.

She tried to twist her face away from his kisses, groaning as she felt his lips brush her throat, his breath warm against her skin. She needed him so much! Their mouths met, hungrily, roughly, and she pulled back, whispering, 'No, no, no. . . .' He used his strength to hold her still, forcing his will on hers. He kissed her again, more gently this time, and she felt her body begin to melt in his arms, her limbs becoming langourous.

'It's been such a long time,' he said, his voice ragged. 'I've thought about nothing but you, Susie.'

'I don't believe you.' But the accusation was also a plea for more reassurance. He was tugging at the buttons of her top as their lips met, exchanging touch for words. She clung to him, her breasts tight against his chest, drowning in his kiss.

'Come.' He pulled her under the bedclothes, out of the cold, the linen whispering against their naked skins. She lay back on the pillow, trembling, as he stared down at her. 'This bed suits you,' he said, drawing his finger down the line of her throat. 'You suit lace and roses. You're the most feminine woman I've ever known.' She arched as he caressed the curves of her breasts, her nipples rigid against his fingers.

'Wolf——'

'You *have* put on weight,' he grinned, his smile a glint of white in the semi-darkness. 'In all the right places.'

'Why did you leave me for so long?' she gasped, closing her eyes as his hand trailed fire down her stomach. 'What happened to you? You just left me in that cell, and I never saw you again——'

'I was in Germany by the time you were rescued. Had things to do.' His lips were possessive, authoritative. 'I knew you'd be safe within a few hours.'

She stopped his hand with both of hers, wanting to talk before this sweet fire engulfed her mind completely.

'What do you *mean*, you knew I'd be safe?' she demanded in a shaky whisper.

'Later,' he commanded, leaning over her to kiss her breasts with warm lips.

'Did you have anything to do with the police finding me?' she asked, incredulity making the words come slowly. He didn't answer, and she sat up, her heart pounding heavily. 'You *did*! It wasn't Draco who informed to the police—it was you!'

'If that's what you want to believe.' But she did believe it—more, she knew it, knew with some unexplained female instinct.

'The police said it was Draco who informed,' she said hesitantly. She was trying to remember what they'd told her. 'They had a telephone call, giving them the place where I was being kept. All the gang were going to be at a meeting in a place called Varese, so the farmhouse would be deserted. . . . So *someone* must have tipped the police off.'

'Someone tipped the police off,' he agreed calmly. 'And Draco took the credit.'

'Then it *was* you! But why?' she demanded, stunned. 'For God's sake, why did you betray the others?'

'Because things had come to a head.' He stroked her cheek, and she strained to see his face. 'What happened between you and me that morning was inevitable. But it was also a big mistake. We wouldn't have been able to go on as before—one of us would have gone crazy. Also,' he shrugged, 'Senta was in a bloodthirsty rage. I knew it wouldn't be long before she organised another "accident"—this time with fatal consequences. And I couldn't watch over you all the time.'

'So you sold them all down the river?' she asked in disbelief.

'I had to get you back to freedom,' he said flatly. 'I couldn't find any other way to protect you. And I couldn't stand the thought of you being cooped up in that cage another day.'

'I don't understand,' she said dazedly. 'What about all your political beliefs? What about all those masses you were supposed to be liberating?'

'I told you,' he smiled, 'I don't expect you to understand. I'd advise you to not even try.'

'Wolf.' She dug her nails into his arm, a new vision thrilling her. 'Can't you see this changes everything? If the police know it was you who set me free, they'll treat you leniently. Maybe even let you go. You've got to give yourself up——'

'No.' His voice was harsh. 'I've got too much still to do.'

'What?' she pleaded. 'More killings? Oh, darling, this is the only way! You can't run for ever—and I want you so much!'

'Hush now.' He kissed her lips shut. 'This is something you can't do anything about, Susie.'

'You'll end up dead,' she said, her heart breaking inside her. 'I know you will. It's your only chance, Wolf. You said just now you were tired of running, that you wanted to give it all up—didn't you?'

He didn't answer, just pulled her close. She closed her eyes, trying to face the new knowledge

in her head. *He* had set her free. Wolf, not Draco.
For her sake, he had betrayed his comrades and
his ideals. Wicked ideals, and wicked comrades,
but ones that had been important to him. The
rights and wrongs of it didn't make sense to her,
but a deep, wonderful gladness was swelling inside
her. He'd cared about her enough to throw
everything away for her sake.

If only she could save him now! Wolf in prison
was a terrible thought, but not as terrible as Wolf
dead, Wolf on the run for the rest of his life.

He didn't give Susie a chance to start arguing
again, though. This time, when he reached for her,
his passion was so fiercely demanding that there
was no room for thought. The ache for him spread
through her like a wildfire, obliterating all else. As
before, in the grass of Lombardy, his name was
the only word that meant anything to her, the only
word she could say. Their bodies twined in
flickering arabesques, linking and unlinking as
desire swept them together. He was a supremely
expert lover, his kisses and caresses tantalising her,
tormenting her, until she felt she could bear no
more, the very blood turning to molten gold in her
veins. Then he took her, thrusting deep into her,
so that she cried out helplessly, her body arching
to accept his love.

'You're mine,' he said roughly. He kissed her
mouth with almost cruel passion. 'Mine, Susie.
You always will be.'

'Don't leave me,' she begged, giddy in his arms.
His weight on her was sweet, fulfilling. 'I couldn't
bear that, Wolf, not again. . . .'

He made love to her with power and control,
using his body to exalt them beyond anything
she'd ever dreamed possible; until, at the towering

height of their passion, the world exploded into an intensity of experience that went beyond her senses—as though, for those long, shuddering seconds, their very souls had mingled and become one fiery being.

Susie came down to earth gasping, her body feeling as though it had been broken on a wheel. 'Easy,' he was murmuring softly, caressing her face, 'take it easy, my love.' Slowly her shaking subsided, the waves of their lovemaking still expanding through her body, fading into a crimson afterglow. 'You,' he said, shaking his head slowly. 'Wonderful, unbelievable you!' He tried to come out of her, but she dug her nails into his back imperiously.

'Stay,' she commanded. She couldn't bear to relinquish him yet, not when the prospect of losing him forever yawned so horribly close.

He kissed the tears on her cheeks, tears she didn't even know she'd shed.

'When will I see you again?' she whispered, knowing he'd tell her the truth now.

'I don't know.' She could see the dark pupils of his eyes staring into hers. 'It may be a long, long time. It may be never.'

'I don't know if I could stand living like that,' she said unevenly. But the wonder of here and now was so precious to her that everything else seemed unreal. Death and violence and flight were unreal. So was Joe, her career, everything in the world that lay outside their two beings.

'We've only got tonight,' she breathed. His body was still hard inside her, and she arched against him slowly, inviting his love again. And as he surged into her, the long, slow waves beginning to take her higher and higher, she clung to him the

way she might have clung to a raft in an endlessly
wide sea, whispering, 'Love me, Wolf, love
me. . . .'

The insistent ringing of the doorbell aroused her
from a fathoms-deep sleep. At first she could
hardly remember who she was or where she was;
then, in a sudden panic, she sat up. The space
beside her was empty. The doorbell shrilled on.

She scrambled out of bed, tugging her dressing-
gown over her nakedness, and dashed through into
the living room. Wolf's clothes were gone. She
opened the door with shaking fingers, and peered
out. The Special Branch man she privately called
Eyebrows was standing on the doorstep, smiling
tolerantly.

'All right, Miss Cheyne? Only it's nearly ten.'

'Y-yes,' she stammered, running her fingers
through her tumbled hair. The realisation that he
had only come to see if she was all right stilled her
wildly beating heart. 'I'm sorry. I must—must
have overslept.'

'Been celebrating finishing your report?'

'I'm afraid so,' she smiled weakly, grasping at
the excuse.

'Right then. Sorry to have disturbed you.' She
watched him walk down the stairs, then went back
inside.

In a kind of daze, she walked through the flat.
The dishes had been washed, the table cleared. The
beer can was in the bin. Even the impromptu bed
she'd made on the sofa, and which had never been
used, had been put away. It was almost as though
Wolf had never been. He'd probably even wiped
his fingerprints off everything he'd touched. She
huddled into her gown, feeling an arctic wind

blowing around her heart, and wandered back to the bedroom, knowing she was hunting for some sign of him, however insignificant. Then she caught sight of the scrap of paper on the bedside table. She snatched it up. There was only one sentence on it—*'don't marry Joe'*.

She sank down on to the bed, dissolving into bitter tears. The man she loved, the terrorist, was gone. What did she have with him, apart from the love they'd shared? Nothing but a feeling as though their two hearts were chained together. She knew nothing about him, only that he was a criminal and a murderer. And now he was gone again, on his own admission maybe for ever. The hopelessness of it was so infinitely depressing. . . .

When she'd cried the worst of her grief out, she showered, scrubbing herself as though to rinse every trace of him off her. Never again, she was swearing to herself, her mood dangerously bitter. She was never going to let Wolf do this to her again. No more heartache, no more fear.

Self-anger made her scrub her delicate skin punishingly hard. She'd been too prissy to sleep with Joe, decent, tender Joe who loved her dearly—and at Wolf's first call she'd been more than ready, purring like an alley-cat under his caresses. What did that tell her about herself? 'You're a rotten hypocrite, Susan Cheyne,' she accused herself fiercely.

She stepped out of the shower, towelling her hair viciously. 'I *will* marry Joe,' she gritted. 'If he'll have me, I *will*!' She walked out of the bathroom, her tanned body still wet and glistening, and picked up the telephone. A vision of deep green eyes flashed into her mind, but she shook it away savagely. It was ten-thirty. She could just make the eleven-fifteen train up to Fairbourne, and be with Joe until Monday. And get Wolf out of her system for ever. She rang the Institute, and got Joe's secretary, Sharleen.

'I'm sorry, Miss Cheyne,' the Welsh voice fluted, 'Dr Dowson's not in at present. He's out in the launch with Mr Evans and Miss Lawrence, collecting samples. I believe they're going to be busy the whole week-end.'

'Oh,' Susie said, disappointment making her damp skin shiver miserably.

'Apparently a tanker's spilled some oil, and they have to see how serious it is. Can I take a message?'

She chewed on the corner of her towel, dismissing the idea of going up on the off-chance of seeing him. He'd be far too busy to bother with her. 'Oh, just tell him I rang.'

'I will, Miss Cheyne.'

'And ask him to call me back when he's got a moment,' she concluded. 'Please? Thanks, Sharleen.'

Feeling empty, she went back to the bedroom. The bed, still unmade, was tumbled, its frothy lace trimmings like stilled sea-foam. The memory of the way Wolf had loved her last night abruptly flooded her mind. She felt her stomach-muscles clench in a spasm of longing and desire, and had to sit down hastily to spare her wobbly knees.

'Damn,' she moaned, hitting the bed with her clenched fist. 'Damn everything!' She knew she was going to spend most of the week-end crying.

And then, without warning, a wave of nausea rose in her, convulsive and uncontrollable. She ran to the bathroom, white-faced. There was nothing in her stomach, but the sickness wouldn't let her go. She hung over the basin, shaking and retching helplessly. After long, long minutes, the nausea receded slightly. She washed her face, feeling wretched to her soul, and stood up to look at herself in the mirror. Haunted, dark-blue eyes stared out at her. She'd been sick like this on Thursday, too.

She went back to the telephone, and made an appointment to see her doctor at the local clinic on Monday. She told the secretary that it was for a routine check-up. She'd been telling herself the same thing, not allowing herself to consider the alternatives. She was due her period about now, but there was no sign of it.

There'd been no sign of the last one, either.

That had been predictable, according to Dr Welch—the shock of her ordeal could easily have disrupted her body's normal functioning. Dr Welch had no reason to suspect that anything else might have caused the same thing.

The week-end was a desert of loneliness. Monday dawned rainy, promising a bleak autumn. She went to the surgery, taking the sample she knew the doctor would need. The doctor, who was well aware of Susie's recent traumas, was reassuringly jolly. She took samples from her, and checked her over—especially her eyes—carefully.

'You look amazingly fit,' she smiled, 'but the tan's deceptive. You could well have a touch of anaemia, especially if you're not eating the right things. I'll rush these samples to the hospital, and let you know the results as soon as I can. All right?'

'All right,' Susie said, trying to smile more cheerfully than she was feeling. She rang Joe that evening, and let him do most of the talking, just drinking in the soothing sound of his voice, and longing for the comfort of someone's arms—but whose she could not say.

On Wednesday the doctor rang Susie back, asking her to come into the surgery that morning. She went with a sinking heart. The doctor was still jolly, but this time her eyes were careful. Somehow, Susie knew what was coming.

'You've turned up a surprise,' she informed Susie. 'Do sit down. We've had the results back; your blood shows a little anaemia, but nothing serious. Tell me, did you have any reason for coming to see me the day before yesterday—apart from feeling a little under the weather?'

'Yes,' Susie said quietly. 'I did have a reason.'

'I see.' The doctor stared at her for a second, then passed her the hospital report to read. 'Well, I'm afraid there's no doubt at all, Susie. The other sample proved positive. You're pregnant.'

CHAPTER TEN

SHOCK kept her numb all the way back to the flat. She sank on to her bed, her hands clasping her abdomen unconsciously, as though she could already feel the life that was starting there. She was going to have a child. His child.

'God,' she whispered, 'I'm going to be a mother.' Herself a mother! And yet—and yet the idea didn't seem as insane to her as it might have done a few months ago. The maturity that she'd earned so painfully was supporting her now. She had changed, permanently and profoundly, and the man who had worked that change was also the father of the child she was going to have. For a second or two tears hovered at the back of her throat, and she gulped them back. Crying wasn't going to help now.

She stared down at her own slender stomach. Yes, she was ready for motherhood, both physically and emotionally. But dear Heaven, if only she could have had this child in the security and happiness of a proper relationship! She didn't care about marriage—if only Wolf could be with her, if only he were anything other than the killer he was! The doctor had been soothing. She'd promised Susie all the help she might need. 'Anything you want,' she'd emphasised meaningfully.

'Like what?' Susie had retorted numbly. No, she didn't need help. Not the sort of help the doctor had hinted at. She was going to have this baby. It

was all she'd have left of Wolf. A sudden joy
surprised her. Even if she never saw him again,
she'd always have his child to love and cling to—
as she would have loved and clung to Wolf, had
things been otherwise.

The thought was immensely cheering, sweeping
away the melancholy and loneliness that had hung
over her for days. 'We've got to start planning,'
she murmured, as though the unborn child could
hear her. But first of all, there were people who
had to be told. And that wasn't going to be easy.

In fact, very little was going to be easy from
now on.

'Pregnant?' Joe stared at her in total shock. His
face blurred as her eyes filled with tears for him,
and she nodded, unable to speak for the lump in
her throat. How much this was going to hurt him,
God alone knew. She'd have given anything to
have been able to spare him the news. But he had
to know. 'Wolf's child?'

'Yes,' she whispered.

'I can't believe it!' Suddenly, as though he had
shrunk in the past second, Joe huddled into his
overcoat. October was chilly, and Grosvenor
Square was windswept, armies of yellow and
brown leaves whirling around them under the
trees. They walked slowly towards the cold white
bulk of the Roosevelt Monument. She fought back
her tears as best she could, clinging to Joe's arm.
Predictably, his first thought was of someone else.
'Have you told your father?'

'Not yet,' she said. She was dreading that more
than anything, and that, too, had to be faced very
soon.

They sat on one of the benches, facing the

marble monument with its bronze-inlaid messages of hope—*Freedom from Want ... Freedom of Worship*. ... She glanced at Joe's face. It was as pale as Roosevelt's, his eyes blank and unseeing behind the gold-rimmed spectacles.

'And you?' he asked quietly, not looking at her. 'How do you feel about it?'

She leaned against him, shutting her eyes. She felt a strange, deep peace inside, and that was the literal truth. Whether it was the peace of despair, or of dangerous hysteria, she had no way of knowing. But though there was anguish in her, it was for others, and not for herself.

'I feel so desperately sorry, Joe. Not for myself—for you and my father. And, in a crazy way, for the baby. I don't dare think of what you must be going through, and as for Dad——'

'Never mind us,' he said, his voice sharp and thin. 'I'm asking how *you* feel about the pregnancy, Susie. I mean, you were more than half in love with the man, weren't you? Surely you must be glad now that you're going to have his child?'

'It isn't that simple,' she said gently. 'This baby will never have a father. It will be a loner, like Wolf. And I don't love Wolf, I never have done.' Hadn't she? Her heart challenged her angrily, but she went on steadily, mindful of the oath she'd sworn never to let him affect her again. 'What happened between me and Wolf was the product of a unique situation, Joe. A one-in-a-million chance. I can't hate the baby because it's half mine, but I'm not exactly delirious about the prospect of being an unmarried mother.' Her beautiful mouth twisted bitterly into a smile, and she pushed her blowing hair back with a gloved hand to look at him. 'I can see I'm shocking you, Joe. I've always shocked you, right from the start. Am I taking all this too calmly?'

'I don't know. How's one supposed to take bombshells like this?' A woman walked past with a shivering borzoi on a leash, and they both watched the dog in silence. 'Tell me,' he went on, 'what would you do if Wolf came back into your life?' She stiffened involuntarily, but he didn't notice. 'If he just arrived one day, and claimed the child. Asked you to go and live with him in Palestine, or wherever people like Wolf can live freely. What would you do?'

'The child is not Wolf's to claim,' she said sharply, surprising herself with the force of her own reaction. 'It's *mine*, Joe. It always will be!'

'Then you're going to have it, after all?' he asked. She could feel his body shivering inside his too-large overcoat, and she looked into his eyes carefully, not quite believing what he was suggesting.

'What do you mean?' she asked.

'I mean you don't *have* to have it,' he said. His eyes moved restlessly away from hers. 'Under the circumstances there isn't a hospital in the country that would refuse you a termination.'

Susie pulled her arm out from under his. It was her turn to be shocked.

'Joe!'

'You don't mean you haven't thought of a termination?' he challenged.

'The child is mine,' she repeated, suddenly seeing him as a completely new person, a stranger to her in every way. 'It isn't some alien thing inside me, like—like a *disease*. It's my baby, and I'm going to have it, Joe.' She shook her head, silencing what he was about to say. 'There's no question of an abortion! I wasn't forced, I'm not ill, the baby's not going to be abnormal in any way. I'm going to have it!'

'I had no idea you had such moral scruples,' he said drily. 'In this day and age——'

Dr Welch flashed into her mind, encouraging her to forget her scruples about sex. It was an odd world, she thought wrily, and morality was one of the oddest things in it.

'I don't know what scruples are,' she replied more gently. 'You know I'm not a pious person. It's just a matter of what we each think is right— and I think it's right for me to have my baby.'

'No matter how much pain and distress you cause others?' he asked, his eyes searching hers. 'And I don't just mean me. I mean your father. This may break his heart, Susie.'

'My father's tougher than that,' she observed wrily. 'You haven't met him! Joe, my child is more important than anyone else's feelings. I know that sounds terribly harsh, but that's the way it is.' She knew she'd never be able to make him understand. Being pregnant had somehow set her apart from everyone else in the world; maybe only another mother-to-be would understand. But she had to try. 'Besides, I could never make a decision like that on my own. The baby is Wolf's, too.'

'He doesn't have any damned rights in this,' Joe said angrily.

'Yes, he does,' she said steadily. 'And so does the baby. It's *alive*, Joe. What would you say if *you* were the father?'

'I'd be asking you to marry me,' he said instantly. She touched his face tenderly, wondering what was going on in his mind.

'As it is?' she probed softly. 'What are you saying?'

'I don't know,' he confessed in anguish. 'I love you, Susie! But I don't know if I'm a big enough person to accept Wolf's son. . . .'

'It may be a daughter,' she smiled.

'It'll be a son,' he retorted acidly. 'If it's Wolf's, it'll be a son. Tell me,' he said, watching her face intently, 'what would you do if it was Wolf asking you to terminate this pregnancy?'

Susie looked away unhappily. That was an ugly question, and she had no ready answer to it.

'I see,' Joe said heavily, interpreting her silence. 'So you still care for him, after all.' He sighed. 'I'm going to need time to think this over, Susie. Not long. Just a few days—just to get my feelings sorted out.'

'Of course,' she nodded. But in her heart she knew she could never accept an offer of marriage from him now, not even to provide a father for the child. She hated herself for the thought, but she was praying he would decide he couldn't marry her, and spare her the pain of refusing him. . . . He reached out, and tugged the muffler loose from around her throat, studying her face with wry, sad eyes.

'Dear God, you're lovely! You're blooming, Susie. I've never seen anyone looking so beautiful.' He hesitated. 'How does it feel? Physically, I mean?'

She laughed quietly. 'You really want to know?'

'Yes,' he nodded, his smile a grimace. 'Just for scientific reasons.'

'I get sick every second or third morning,' she admitted, thinking of the retching miseries she regularly went through. 'That'll probably go away later on—I hope. I sleep incredibly deeply, I don't know why.' She pushed her hands into her pockets, and stared across the leaf-strewn park, wondering with an inner ache where Wolf was now, what he was doing. She should be telling all this to him. 'My breasts tingle. I think they're getting bigger, actually, but that may just be because I eat ravenously. The doctor says that in a month I can expect to start losing my waistline.' She shrugged, running out of symptoms, running out of ways to tell him how she felt inside. 'There's not much difference yet. I'm still trim and maidenly.'

'There will be a difference. I can just see you staggering around with a great tummy,' he nodded, his eyes still full of a remote sadness. Suddenly she knew that he would never be able to marry her. He needed some plain, ordinary girl who would support him and adore him—not a wild gull like herself, bearing another man's child in her womb, and another man's image in her heart. And as if he'd picked up her thought, he sighed heavily.

'Even if I did persuade you to terminate the pregnancy for my sake, you could never love me afterwards—could you?' He didn't wait for an answer, but stood up quickly, huddling into his coat with that same shrunken movement. She rose to face him, feeling in her bones that this was goodbye. 'You'd better get yourself and your baby into the warm,' he advised. 'It's going to be a wild winter.' His face was looking pinched and old, and on impulse she flung her arms round him, hugging him tight. What would have happened if it hadn't been for Comrade Wolf? Would she have come back and married this man, made him a good, loyal wife? There was no answer. Fate had decided otherwise.

They were alike, she and Joe. Both alone, both sentenced to love the unobtainable.

She was about to cry again, and she didn't want to hear him say goodbye. She kissed his cheek blindly, and ran back across the park, the wind catching in her piebald hair and whipping it across her wet cheeks.

She came out of the committee-meeting feeling shaken but triumphant. Her report had had a stormy hearing, and the Department of the Environment had been represented by a very sharp-witted troubleshooter. But even he, after he'd heard Susie's evidence, had been forced to admit that the subject of coastal pollution needed serious attention. A watchdog committee, at the very least, would be on the way soon. It had been a triumph not only for her, but also for the International Geophysical Committee as a whole.

'If you play your cards right,' James Ormerod said confidentially as they emerged into the common-room where tea was being laid out, 'the present government might ask you to serve on a Quango aimed at dealing with the coastal pollution problem. That'll be a feather in your cap, eh?'

'It would indeed.' She smiled at the sixty-year-old head of the Institute, thinking of the baby inside her. The thought that she might have to turn down an offer like that would have driven her mad a few months ago. Now, she didn't care.

'Splendid report,' one of the committee members told her enthusiastically, pressing tea and cake on her. 'You've started the ball rolling now, Miss Cheyne.'

'I was just telling her she might be in line for membership of the next Quango,' James Ormerod nodded, bustling off again. The conversation was general and enthusiastic, most of the people who'd been at the meeting delighted with the effect Susie's report had had.

'What did I tell you,' James hissed importantly, returning up to take Susie's arm. 'The government chappie wants a word with you!'

He led her excitedly over to the Department of the Environment troubleshooter, who was chewing cake vigorously in majestic solitude at the other end of the room.

'I'll leave you two to talk,' James said, effacing himself diplomatically. The government man was a shrewd-looking person in his late thirties, and he nodded briskly at Susie, clever eyes probing hers.

'Very concise report, Miss Cheyne.'

'Thank you,' she said calmly. 'I hope you're going to do something about it.'

'Up to the Minister,' he replied. 'I shall be conveying your main points to his secretary this afternoon. Government's a collection of ladders,' he said with an unexpected smile. 'But if an idea climbs briskly enough, it might just make it to the top. There was something I wanted to show you, though.' He had a copy of *The Times* under his arm, and now he passed it to her. 'I brought this for you. Article on the front page might interest you.' It was ringed in red ink. She studied it with growing intentness. The headline read 'KIDNAP VICTIM FREED.' Underneath it, the story began, *'Maria Dietrich, 16-year old daughter of Austrian politician Ingrid Dietrich, was returned to her mother alive and well on Wednesday night after a three-month kidnap ordeal, it was revealed today. Maria disappeared whilst on a school holiday in Italy in June. It is believed that she was kidnapped by the notorious Alba Rossa, who were also responsible for the kidnapping of 22-year-old Briton Susan Cheyne in July, but it is not known where Maria was being held, or how she was found. Madame Dietrich, a widow, had made an urgent plea to the world press agencies not to give the story any publicity. Seven people have been detained for questioning by the French police in connection with the kidnapping, and Interpol were last night claiming a major breakthrough in the hunt for the terrorist gang's leaders.'*

Susie stared at the print, unseeing. So there had been another tenant in another tiny grey prison! Her heart went out to the freed girl. At only sixteen, she must have suffered more than Susie herself could ever have done—and she'd been in their hands a full month longer.

'Rumour has it in government circles,' the troubleshooter observed, sipping his tea, 'that Alba Rossa's finished.'

'Finished?' she repeated, feeling a chill strike into her heart.

'Yes. Unofficial, mind you, but I'm telling you because you're one of the few people who've got an immediate right to know. They've captured the entire outfit.' He frowned at her. 'You don't look very pleased.'

'I'm delighted.' But she was thinking of Wolf. Was he in the net, too? Resolutely, she crushed all pity. Killers like Wolf deserved all they got. 'Poor kid,' she went on, 'I bet her mother was nearly mad with fear.'

'Indeed. Ingrid Dietrich is a very important person in the Austrian government. You were picked for financial reasons, this girl Maria for political ones. Hasn't done them much good, though, has it?'

'No,' Susie said vaguely, 'I suppose it hasn't.'

'Keep the paper,' he invited as she offered it back to him. She nodded thanks, and pushed it into her handbag. Someone else had come up to congratulate her on her report, and she was swept off into another series of conversations, the subject of Maria Dietrich sliding to the back of her mind.

Brown-Shoes followed her home in the afternoon. Outside her flat, he came up to her, holding a copy of *The Sun*.

'Read the paper, Miss Cheyne?'

'Yes,' she nodded, thinking of that tiny grey jail again. 'I didn't even know the girl had been kidnapped.'

'Nobody did. There was a complete news blackout.' Brown-Shoes was looking satisfied. 'Word is, they've got the lot. Shouldn't wonder if we were to be taken off your back pretty shortly.'

She grinned, her eyes sparkling deep blue. 'I shall miss you. Not every girl can boast a man following her wherever she goes!'

She walked to the bottom of the stairs.

'Miss Cheyne,' he called.

She turned, still smiling. 'Yes?'

'I think you have a visitor upstairs.' She stared at him, her eyes narrowed, but he was already walking back to his Rover. Did he mean her father? Puzzled, she went up to the flat and opened her door, peering inside curiously. Her heart jolted wildly as she saw him, relaxed on her sofa.

'Wolf!' She slammed the door shut, behind her, leaning against it for support. 'You got away!'

He held up the skeleton key he'd used before, his smile wry.

'A last return to my wicked ways. I'm sorry if I startled you.' He rose fluidly, green eyes laughing at her incredulity. 'You look wonderful. How did your report go?'

'Why are you here?' she asked, bewilderment making her giddy. There was something different about him; his clothes, she realised suddenly, were part of it. He was in an exquisitely cut charcoal suit, his tie dark against a snowy silk shirt. That sense of violence in him had been transformed into the dangerous elegance of a superbly handsome man of wealth and breeding.

He took her in his arms. The first touch of his mouth had her shaking, her fingers digging into his back as though to reassure herself that he was real.

'I've come back for you,' he said softly. The depths of his eyes were clear and bright—but no longer cool and indifferent. There was a warmth in them that melted her bones, made her want to dissolve into him.

'The Special Branch man knows you're here,' she said, remembering in sudden panic. 'You've got to run——'

'Hush.' He kissed her parted lips, holding her still. 'I'm not running anywhere any more, Susie. It's all over.'

'But——' she choked.

'I'm not what you think I am,' he said, cutting through her stammered protests. There was still a smile in the tails of his eyes, as though he was finding something deeply amusing. 'Last time I saw you, I told you I had work to do.' He picked the copy of *The Times* out of her bag, and pointed to the article ringed in red. 'I finished it on Wednesday.'

She stared at the story. 'KIDNAP VICTIM FREED'.

'*You?*' she asked in disbelief. 'Oh, dear God. . . .' She swayed against him, her mind turning upside down. 'Are you a policeman?'

'No.' He led her to the sofa, seeing that her legs were about to give way. 'Not exactly.'

She stared up into the harshly beautiful, tanned face. 'What, then?' she whispered, feeling as though she were in a dream.

'I run an international security firm, Susie. It's based in Vienna, but it has branches throughout Europe. There's one here in London. It's called Santanya Securities.' He took her hand, caressing her slender fingers with his own. 'My name is Wolf Santanya. The first half is German, the second half's Spanish.' He smiled, laughter-lines etched at the corners of his eyes. 'But I'm Austrian.'

'Ingrid Dietrich,' Susie said numbly. 'She's Austrian——'

'Ingrid is my only sister,' he said quietly. 'Maria is her only daughter. When she was kidnapped in June, Ingrid was shattered. Her husband Franz died five years ago—like Ingrid, he was a member of the Austrian Government—and she has no one in the world but Maria—apart from me.' He settled back, his eyes holding hers. 'You know how your father suffered.' The quiet, authoritative voice permitted no disbelief; she knew in the core of her heart that he was telling her the truth.

'She must have been distraught,' she said

pityingly. 'To think of her innocent child in the hands of people like that!'

He nodded. 'Alba Rossa were mad dogs, Susie. Not even other terrorist organisations would deal with them. And they had no plans for letting Maria go. Ever. They were going to repeat the Aldo Moro tragedy—keep Maria hidden for several months, issuing photographs and tape-recordings from time to time to keep public interest alive, and then, one day, leave her body in a city street somewhere in Europe. Dead.'

'That's unbelievable,' Susie gasped.

'It's happened before,' he said brutally. 'And it may happen again, if madmen like Alba Rossa aren't stopped in time.'

'But how did you get involved?' she demanded, hungry for information to fill the void inside her.

'I volunteered,' he said simply. 'To go underground, penetrate the terrorist network, and find Maria, if possible.'

'But how could you?' Susie gasped. 'You weren't a spy or anything——'

'Exactly,' he said with a grim smile. 'Which meant I was a new face. No files on me existed anywhere. Secondly, I know about things like self-defence and security. Guns, bombs, booby-traps. They're my business, though I'm usually on the other side, trying to work out ways of stopping people from using them in banks and public places. Thirdly——' He raised his shoulders wrily. 'I was a university student in the 1970s. That gives my age away. But that meant I had some knowledge of the sort of background many urban terrorists had—I knew the jargon, the slogans. I could quote Lenin and Marcuse and Angela Davis. I could "remember" famous protests and

demonstrations. And fourthly—I had a strong
enough motive to make me want to go underground in search of Maria. I love Ingrid, Susie.
And I love my niece. She's the sweetest child,
gentle as a butterfly. And to think of her in the
hands of those murderers——' For a second, his
eyes glinted the ruthless icy green she'd seen so
many times before, and she felt fear touch her
spine.

'Don't,' she begged him. 'You terrify me when
you look like that.'

'My love,' he smiled, kissing her tenderly. 'You
never had anything to fear from me. But if only
you knew what a damned headache you were to
me!'

'How?' she asked.

'By presenting me with a very serious distraction.
Penetrating Alba Rossa took remarkably little
time, because of one lucky, tragic, break. The
death of Johann Weiss.'

'You didn't kill him?' Susie asked fearfully, half-
dreading that the answer might be yes.

'No,' he said gently. 'I knew Johann. He was a
brave man. His death was a terrible accident. He
was training a bomb-disposal squad outside
Zurich when a parcel of explosives was accidentally
detonated. I claimed to have murdered him, and
the Swiss security police backed the story up from
their side.' He winced. 'It was ugly, but it's an ugly
game. I feel somehow Johann would have
approved. And that got me into Alba Rossa more
effectively than any cover could have done.'

Susie closed her eyes. He wasn't a killer. It was
as though heavy iron chains had just dropped off
her mind, the relief sharp and wonderful. 'Did you
find out where Maria was?' she asked, fascinated

as well as appalled by the horrible danger he'd been through.

'No. Alba Rossa was a very small organisation, but a very tight one. It was split into two sections, the Executive Committee and the Subordinate Committee. A high degree of secrecy operated right through the organisation—none of us were supposed to know where or who the others were, which made my task even harder. The Subordinate Committee's function was to raise money and recruit new members. But at the time I'd penetrated the organisation, the Subordinate Committee were already planning to kidnap you. I was faced with a very painful dilemma—whether to leave another innocent person to their tender mercies, and keep on the track of Maria, or whether to stay with the new kidnap victim and watch over her.'

'You decided to stay with me?' she said softly. The picture was slowly beginning to make sense to her now. 'I remember Senta saying you'd taken over the whole operation at the last minute.'

'Yes.' He picked up the skeleton key and toyed with it, his gaze far away. 'Senta had been the leader up till then, and I couldn't protect you properly from the little sadist unless I assumed leadership myself. She was in a cold fury at being supplanted—and I had to find some way of defusing that, for your sake.'

'By becoming her lover?' Susie asked, pain lancing through her heart.

'Occasionally,' Wolf Santanya nodded, his eyes sombre. 'I'm not going to deny that to you, Susie. But I want you to know that it was never anything but a very ugly duty.'

'Poor you,' Susie retorted, unable to keep the

angry edge out of her voice. She was having a
painful vision of Senta's tennis-star body pressing
against Wolf that morning in the sun.

'Susie.' He reached for her hand, but she pulled
away sharply, bitterly hurt by the thought of Wolf
making love to Senta, giving Senta his desire for
all those weeks. 'Susie,' he said more gently, 'it
wasn't the way you think. With Senta it was short,
sharp and nasty. Something I hated, body and
soul. Something which also became more and
more impossible as I began to care more about
you. I've never in my life known anything like the
way you and I make love.'

'Sure,' she said tersely. 'So what happened
then?'

'Well,' he replied, watching her with compassion
in his leopard's eyes, 'I simply had to pray that
there would be time to find Maria before they did
anything to her. The news blackout was crucial—
without publicity, Alba Rossa's plan was useless,
and they were in a quandary for several weeks.
That period of hesitation saved Maria's life.'

'Where was she being kept?'

'In a luxury apartment in Milan. After you
were freed, I wasn't simply pretending to be on the
run—I was quite literally being hunted by half the
police forces of Europe. That meant that Alba
Rossa were totally against my making contact with
the Executive Committee, in case I led the dogs
there. Very few people knew that I was an agent,
because that was the way we'd planned it at the
outset. And it was a long, hard trail to Maria. It
led me to Germany, then to Northern Ireland. I
spent that night at your flat on my way to Belfast.
And then, in the end, I got to the famous
Executive Committee—four frightened middle-

class youngsters, posing with guns in a luxury flat
in a quiet Milan suburb.'

'How is she?' Susie asked, fearing the answer.

'Amazingly well,' he said, wonderment in his
tone. 'Shocked, lonely, and thin—but unharmed
physically or mentally. Perhaps not even Alba
Rossa could find it in their hearts to hurt Maria.
You can imagine how joyful she is to be reunited
with her mother.'

'Yes,' Susie said, feeling a lump in her throat.
Sympathy for Ingrid and Maria Dietrich was
helping her to reconcile herself to the thought of
Wolf and Senta. 'Yes, I can.' She pressed her palms
into her eyes, feeling the unreality roll over her
again. 'This is all too crazy to be happening. I keep
thinking I'm going to wake up, and find it was all a
dream, and you're still a terrorist on the run.' For
the first time since she'd walked into the flat, the
other things in her life began to surface in her mind.
This man before her was the father of her child! She
stood up, and walked to the window, keeping a tight
rein on her battered emotions.

'What made you decide to get me out of the
farmhouse, Mr Santanya?'

'I told you,' he said calmly, ignoring her cold
use of his surname. 'Things came to head. After
that day on the hillside, when you tried to kill
me——' She winced unhappily at the reference. '——
I knew I was much too involved with you
emotionally to be able to carry on in my role as
"Comrade Wolf", the cold-blooded killer. I almost
told you the whole story that morning, Susie. But I
knew you'd never be able to hide that knowledge—
Senta would have seen through you in a second. I
often wondered whether she was seeing through
me. I arranged a meeting in a nearby town,

Varese, and made contact with the Italian anti-terrorist squad. It was given out that Draco had betrayed them, and the rest of Alba Rossa believed I'd had a lucky escape.'

'I see.' She turned to stare out of the window. Brown-Shoes was sitting in his Rover, reading his copy of *The Sun*. They obviously knew about Wolf now, had perhaps always known. A wave of melancholy came over her. She'd been little more than a pawn in a game of double-bluff and counter-espionage. What was to become of her now? Was she to be left alone, with Wolf's child growing in her womb? 'Tell me,' she said in a strained voice, 'do you have a wife, Mr Santanya?'

'Yes.' His voice was quiet. She closed her eyes to try and keep back the scalding tears. It was all over, then. The long, long journey she'd made into herself, into love, was all over. She shuddered as she felt his hands take her shoulders and draw her back against the warmth of his body. 'Yes,' he said softly, 'I have a wife, Susie. If she'll have me.' She turned to face him, her dark eyes brimming. 'I've come back to ask you to marry me. I love you, Susan Cheyne. I love you more than life itself—and I have done, almost from the first moment I saw you.'

'Oh, Wolf——' She clung to him, the hunger of their kiss making up for all the loneliness, all the misunderstandings, all the pain they'd both been through. Her fingers were knotted in his thick, dark hair, her body shaking in his embrace. 'I adore you,' she gasped between kisses, 'God, how I've missed you! How could you leave me like that, how *could* you?'

'I'll never leave you again,' he swore in a husky voice. 'Will you marry me?'

'Of course I will,' she said tearfully. A laugh bubbled up in her throat. 'How on earth am I ever going to explain this to my father?'

'I have a very good representative doing that right now,' he said tenderly. 'My sister Ingrid. I asked her if she would take Maria to see your father in Zurich, and try and explain the whole thing to him. I think they'll manage to convince him, don't you?'

'I love you,' she said weakly, tracing the tanned lines of his face with wondering fingers. 'You're the most wonderful man in the world. When are we getting married?'

'As soon as humanly possible,' he grinned. 'We've fallen from grace twice already—I'd like the fourth time to be legal, at least.'

'The fourth time?' she queried in amusement.

'Maybe the fourteenth,' he conceded. 'We're flying back to Vienna tomorrow. Both of us. I want you to see my house, and the orchards, and the Danube. I want you to fall in love with Austria, Susie.' He grinned. 'I'm afraid I'm ridiculously wealthy. Can you stand that?'

'It's not as good as being romantically poor,' she smiled in amusement, 'but I think I can stand that, yes.'

'Good,' he nodded. 'We're having dinner at the Ritz tonight.'

'What?' she gaped. 'With my hair like this?'

'You're getting married like that,' he said practically. 'You'll be the admiration of the place. Providing you don't try and strangle me with the napkins.'

'Oh, Wolf,' she said, horror overcoming her as she remembered that savage morning in Lombardy, 'how are you ever going to forgive me for that?'

'It was your murder attempt that convinced me I was going to marry you,' he retorted calmly. 'While you were trying to bring my career to an abrupt end, I was telling myself that if I ever got out of this alive I'd at least know I'd found the only woman in the world who might be a match for me!' He kissed her smiling mouth. 'Call it a retribution for Senta, and we're quits. Yes?'

'I don't know about that,' she growled darkly. 'I'll have to think about it. I'm not sure that you aren't too good a deceiver for me!'

'It was very hard keeping up the pretence with you at times,' he admitted. 'But I did enjoy those arguments we had!'

'I'll bet,' she grinned. 'How you must have been laughing up your sleeve at me! You had me convinced you were the most fanatical killer around. My love, how strange it's going to be, having normal, blissful lives after all we've been through. . . .'

'Roll on normality,' he chuckled. 'We've shared some strange experiences, Susie. That makes us unique, and binds us together for ever.'

'Poor Joe,' she sighed obliquely, thinking of the sorrow of those brown eyes in Grosvenor Square.

'Yes,' he said gently. 'Poor Joe. He's lost the most marvellous woman on earth, and he knows it.'

'You know so much more about me than I do about you,' she said in a soft voice. 'I simply know that you're the man I love, and that I'd trust you with my soul. But I'm aching to learn about the way you live, and the things you do for fun, and what you like for breakfast, and what sort of music you like——'

'Mozart, naturally,' he said, kissing her to stop

the flow of questions. 'I like all the simple things in life, my love.' His eyes glinted. 'Fast cars. Gliding. Racehorses. Making love to my wife.'

'Which reminds me,' she said suddenly, staring up into the beautiful, wild green eyes that had haunted her for so long, 'what do you think about children?'

'Children?' he repeated, eyebrows arching. 'As soon as possible, naturally.'

'Oh,' she said, joy surging up in her like a hundred fountains exploding into life. 'Oh. That's good.' She took his hand, and laid it on the smooth plane of her stomach. 'I've got something to tell you, my love. . . .'

Give the Rose of Romance on Mother's Day.

DESIRABLE PROPERTY
Catherine George

THE ONLY ONE
Penny Jordan

A SUMMER IDYLL
Betty Neels

NEVER IN A LIFETIME
Lilian Peake

Bring someone some romance this Mother's Day. Four brand new titles from Mills and Boon, attractively gift wrapped for £4.40. Look for this gift pack where you buy Mills and Boon romances – it's available from 8th February 1985.

ROMANCE

Next month's romances from Mills & Boon

Each month, you can choose from a world of variety in romance with Mills & Boon. These are the new titles to look out for next month.

SAVE MY SOUL FROM SIN Lindsay Armstrong
WRECKER'S BRIDE Kathryn Cranmer
RING OF CRYSTAL Jane Donnelly
OUT OF WEDLOCK Sandra Field
NEVER KISS A STRANGER Mary Gabriel
THE HABIT OF LOVING Rosemary Hammond
BLUEBEARD'S BRIDE Sarah Holland
THE FLAME TREE Elizabeth Graham
THE PASSIONATE LOVER Carole Mortimer
DRAGON MAN Elizabeth Oldfield
NO TIME FOR MARRIAGE Roberta Leigh
THE ROAD Emma Goldrick

Buy them from your usual paperback stockist, or write to: Mills & Boon Reader Service, P.O. Box 236, Thornton Rd, Croydon, Surrey CR9 3RU, England. Readers in South Africa-write to: Mills & Boon Reader Service of Southern Africa, Private Bag X3010, Randburg, 2125.

Mills & Boon
the rose of romance

ROMANCE

A tempting offer from Mills & Boon

Temptation is a new kind of romance from Mills & Boon. Exciting, sensuous, compelling... written for today's woman. Two new titles will be published every month, starting in February.

SPECIAL INTRODUCTORY PRICE
ONLY 99P EACH

And to make Temptation totally irresistible, the February and March titles can be yours for the special introductory price of just 99p.

Go on – give in to Temptation.

The Rose of Romance

Take 4
Exciting Books
Absolutely
FREE

Love, romance, intrigue... all are captured for you by Mills & Boon's top-selling authors. By becoming a regular reader of Mills & Boon's Romances you can enjoy 6 superb new titles every month plus a whole range of special benefits: your very own personal membership card, a free monthly newsletter packed with recipes, competitions, exclusive book offers and a monthly guide to the stars, plus extra bargain offers and big cash savings.

AND an Introductory FREE GIFT for YOU.
Turn over the page for details.

As a special introduction we will send you four
exciting Mills & Boon Romances Free and
without obligation when you complete
and return this coupon.

At the same time we will reserve a subscription to
Mills & Boon Reader Service for you. Every month,
you will receive 6 of the very latest novels by leading
Romantic Fiction authors, delivered direct to your
door. You don't pay extra for delivery — postage and
packing is always completely Free. There is no
obligation or commitment — you can cancel your
subscription at any time.

You have nothing to lose and a whole world of
romance to gain.

Just fill in and post the coupon today to MILLS & BOON
READER SERVICE, FREEPOST, P.O. BOX 236, CROYDON,
SURREY CR9 9EL.

Please Note:- READERS IN SOUTH AFRICA write to
Mills & Boon, Postbag X3010,
Randburg 2125, S. Africa.

- -

FREE BOOKS CERTIFICATE

**To: Mills & Boon Reader Service, FREEPOST, P.O. Box 236,
Croydon, Surrey CR9 9EL.**

Please send me, free and without obligation, four Mills & Boon Romances, and reserve a
Reader Service Subscription for me. If I decide to subscribe I shall, from the beginning of the
month following my free parcel of books, receive six new books each month for £6.60, post
and packing free. If I decide not to subscribe, I shall write to you within 10 days. The free
books are mine to keep in any case. I understand that I may cancel my subscription at any
time simply by writing to you. I am over 18 years of age.

Please write in BLOCK CAPITALS

Signature _____

Name _____

Address _____

_____ Post code _____

SEND NO MONEY — TAKE NO RISKS.

Please don't forget to include your Postcode.

Remember, postcodes speed delivery. Offer applies in UK only and is not valid
to present subscribers. Mills & Boon reserve the right to exercise discretion in
granting membership. If price changes are necessary you will be notified.

6R *Offer expires June 30th 1985*

EP8